WHERE'S ...

ELI?

To Abby,
With much love.
Hope you enjoy.

WHERE'S ...
ELI?

ANOTHER
BROOKLYN
TALE

of the Al and Mick Forte crime fiction series

ALEX S. AVITABILE

Brooklyn, New York

For information about this title, contact:
Alex S. Avitabile, either via the contact page of the
https://AlandMickForte.net website
or by emailing alex@AlandMickForte.net

Library of Congress Control Number: 2019913001

ISBN Trade Paperback: 978-1-7323063-2-5
ISBN eBook: 978-1-7323063-3-2

Printed in the United States of America

Cover and Interior Design by 1106 Design, LLC

Author photo by Ron Jordan Natoli and Steve Warham of Ron
Jordan Natoli Studio, 352 Court Street, Brooklyn, NY 11231

This book is dedicated to my beloved late wife,
THERESA LIU AVITABILE,
as well as to those close to me who have died
since the publication of *Occupational Hazard:*
my father,
FELIX J. AVITABILE,
my cats,
MACK and PATRICK,
and my friends,
DELORES RIVERA-FERRAR,
MANUELA BOURBEAU,
FR. PATRICK KANE, RICHARD JOYA,
YU CHEN CHIANG and
FR. ANTONIUS HO.

CONTENTS

CHAPTER 1
"My cousin Eli's into some real *pazzo* crap." • *1*

CHAPTER 2
"Be a pal and do me a real solid." • *8*

CHAPTER 3
"Looks like every single one of your accounts
has been cleaned out." • *14*

CHAPTER 4
"There's no money there!" • *20*

CHAPTER 5
"It will take us awhile to get to the bottom of this." • *24*

CHAPTER 6
"We're going to need Julius's assistance." • *29*

CHAPTER 7
"Light every … candle in sight." • *35*

CHAPTER 8
Feeling terrible. • *47*

CHAPTER 9
"They call it the head-banger." • *58*

CHAPTER 10
"I'm afraid to think of the 'something else' possibility." • *71*

CHAPTER 11
[It] hits the fan on all conceivable fronts. • *77*

CHAPTER 12
Finally, a lead. • *87*

CHAPTER 13
"Stop with the excuses already." • *94*

CHAPTER 14
"Where's … Eli?" • *107*

CHAPTER 15
"Taught Chubby Checker how to do the Twist." • *114*

CHAPTER 16
"Change of the meeting's agenda." • *121*

CHAPTER 17
"Ain't want no publicity." • *127*

CHAPTER 18
"Parking Spot Zorro." • *134*

CHAPTER 19
"An uphill battle." • *141*

CHAPTER 20
"I'm totally overwhelmed." • *154*

CHAPTER 21
"A risk he refuses to accept." • *164*

CHAPTER 22
"We are here for The Matter of Al Forte." • *168*

CHAPTER 23
"It was a thing of beauty." • *191*

CHAPTER 24
The feeling is mutual. • *202*

• • •

Acknowledgements • *210*
About the Author • *213*

CHAPTER 1

"My cousin Eli's into some real *pazzo* crap."

"WHERE'S THAT FUCKIN' asshole Eli?"

"I don't know, Mick. He's supposed to be here by now."

Mick Forte is my cousin. His father and my father are brothers. Eli Ativa is Mick's cousin too, but through their mothers who are sisters. While Eli and I are not related, we may as well be, given the deep connections between Mick's family and mine.

Back in the day, we all grew up near each other on the so-called mean streets of what was referred to then as South Brooklyn, in a close-knit blue-collar neighborhood. Today, our particular part of that neighborhood is called Carroll Gardens. Then, it was solidly working-class Italian with a smattering of some well-to-do folks, consisting of upper middle-class professionals, successful business people, and high-ranking mobsters. Now, it's gentrified, and the newer folks are upwardly mobile and more affluent. The remnants of the past, like Mick's and my parents, are seniors getting by on pensions and social security, but doing all right because they are homeowners and frugal folks, who eat out only on special occasions. The same was true of Eli's parents, all their lives, until they died a few years back.

"That cocksucker had better get his ass here real quick or he's cruisin' for a real nice bruisin'. We gotta figure out how to fix this shit. Don't that *sfaccim* know the kinds a problems he's made for you?"

"This shit" and "the kinds a problems" refer to something that happened a little over a week before this conversation.

"And doncha think I ain't alla sudden not no longer pissed at you, you fuckin' idiot, for not listenin' to what I done friggin' told you I can't not remember how many damn times already about my asshole, good-for-*u' cazz* cousin. This *budell* never ever wudda happened if you weren't such a friggin' jerkoff and stupid nice guy."

Mick had told me, "My cousin Eli's into some real *pazzo* crap and who knows what's squirmin' around in that fat crazy head of his. Stay away from that *strunz*. You see him, say hi, and goodbye. Just walk away, even if he tries to tell you somethin'. You gotta know he's up to nuttin' but no fuckin' good. He comes to your office or house, don't open the door; don't let him in. He gets in, get rid of him; throw him out if you hafta. He calls you on the phone, just hang the fuck up as fast as you can.

"I'm tellin' you the problem with my stinkin' cousin Eli goes back to when he was a kid. His folks spoiled the crap outa him. He could do whatever the fuck he wants, and both his mom and dad never yelled at him for nuttin' no matter what bullshit he's up to.

"Me, my folks knew I'm gonna follow my dad and be a hood, but they had rules and would bust my chops if I ain't obeyed 'em. They also knew I hadda get some schoolin'. I hadda be good with numbers, hadda be able to talk to all kinds a folks, and hadda read good—you know, to keep up with the news and so wisenheimers like you ain't think they could take advantage of me withcha hundred dollar words and the other sly, sneaky shit your smarty-ass kind like to put over on those of us you think ain't got no smarts.

"I skipped school whenever I felt like it, and so did that twerp Eli, but when my folks found out, I'd be slammed. But that *strunz* Eli would go untouched, ain't even got yelled at any. He'd bring home the note from the principal and'd write a letter with some nutso excuse for why he ain't went to school and his folks'd sign it. His mom's only worry was that it was wrote neat. That whacko got away with lots of shit that not even I ain't could."

Mick knows Eli is smart but says he's irresponsible and lazy. I have a different take. Eli is extremely bright, almost genius-like. What many, like Mick, perceive as laziness, is in my estimation boredom. If something interests, excites him, he's inspired, immerses himself in it and it consumes him. However, if something bores him, he barely lifts a finger regardless how important it may otherwise be.

Regarding the matter that had Mick so worked up, Eli had come by my office to ask that I do him a "solid." I was in the midst of a wild scramble to rush out the door for a major closing for which I was already running late. Without any time to give the request much thought, I said okay. I did not even consider Mick's prior warnings. I don't always pay attention to his threats. Mick overreacts at times—and besides, I am an adult, an experienced attorney, and can make my own decisions, even though my wife Theresa constantly implores me to listen carefully to whatever Mick says and to heed his warnings.

Until recently I was extremely reluctant to take any of Mick's advice. As a lawyer, I am bound to adhere to a code of legal ethics. My ability to practice law, my license, depends on my not violating any of its ethical precepts. And, first and foremost, we attorneys are to exercise our independent judgment, based on our knowledge of the law and the code of ethics.

My previous reluctance as to Mick was primarily due to his known affiliation with the Mob, the Mafia, whatever you want to call it. As far as I understood, his law was the law of the streets, not the duly enacted laws of the State of New York or of the U.S. of A.

I was aware that Mick was transitioning more and more to legitimate businesses. Mick's dad, my Uncle Nicola, or Nick as everyone called him, was a loan shark and a bookie. At some point I learned that many of my uncle's generation went into businesses that weren't legitimate by the State's standards, not because of lack of ability, but due to lack of formal education. Poverty prevented many Italian immigrants and their children from getting a good education. Plenty had to drop out of school to work menial jobs to help support their families. While many had innate business sense, they could not obtain the credentials to go into finance and similar fields. Those who knew how to work with money would improvise and, in some cases, become what the law would call loan sharks. These sharks, in truth, would provide funds to fellow immigrants, because they did not have access to the standard lenders, banks and similarly chartered financial institutions.

So, Uncle Nick would make loans to those who the regulated lenders would not serve. While some of the unregulated lenders considered themselves to be, and acted like, outlaws and dealt with those who failed to make timely repayments by resorting to threats and even physical violence, Mick's dad refused to treat his borrowers in that manner. Luckily, Mick's mom, my Aunt Tessie, had a brother who was an attorney, Mick's Uncle Luigi, and Luigi assisted my Uncle Nick to run his loan business similar to the regulated lenders, by taking back collateral, so that upon a default, rather than breaking knee caps or worse, Uncle Nick would foreclose and get repaid either at the foreclosure sale or by taking over the collateral.

Now, this is not to suggest that Uncle Nick's borrowers' loans were only for regular business or personal purposes, to establish businesses or buy properties, including homes. He also made loans to gamblers and to bookies and other members of the criminal class to finance their illicit activities. But without exception, collateral was demanded and upon default duly exercised upon.

Over time, Uncle Nick made out quite well from his loan collections, but also from exercising his rights against the collateral that secured defaulted loans. He would find himself in the property management business, and he would then expand it into his own real estate development business. Mick would follow in his dad's footsteps and eventually take over the businesses Uncle Nick established, and Mick would further grow and expand those businesses and start new ones. Little by little, but initially unbeknownst to me, Mick transitioned to being more a legitimate businessman and less an outlaw.

I also viewed Mick as a loose cannon, as someone who would dive head-on into things without thinking them through. One of the times he tried to help me, he was accused of bribery and threatened with jail, and I faced a potential disciplinary proceeding that could have resulted in the suspension of my law license or even disbarment. Luckily, once the facts became known, it was clear that Mick was simply calling in a favor that was owed to him, and the city official Mick was alleged to have bribed handled it in a way that did not show favoritism toward the client of mine whom Mick was trying to help, and Mick and I were exonerated.

Then, there was this child support proceeding that a former colleague, Mary Woodley, asked me to bring for her against our former boss, Gordon Gilbert, a powerful, devious bully. Gilbert was the head of the law firm Mary and I worked for, a firm from which I was fired. Mary came to me and told me that Gilbert had raped her and fathered a child. Mary was desperate and said I was her last resort in her attempt to get Gilbert, a First Deputy Mayor at the time, to support that child. Gilbert was known to resort to "dirty tricks" to retaliate against those whom he felt did him dirt or those who brought him problems. Mick was well aware of Gilbert's history, learned of the case I was bringing on Mary's behalf, and insisted that I needed his help to handle the "street" aspect of the fight ahead. I initially rejected Mick's offer, but later relented when I found myself in jail for reasons I attributed to Gilbert and due to pressure from Mick and my wife, who was emphatic about my need to augment my "book smarts" with Mick's "street smarts."

In the end, Mary achieved justice largely due to Mick's efforts, which significantly helped me to prevail in the court proceedings I brought on Mary's behalf.

I would eventually realize that Mick is a valuable resource, trustworthy and reliable, and I became much less reluctant to listen to and follow his advice.

Now, as I discover all my bank accounts, including my attorney escrow accounts, have been mysteriously cleaned out, without a blessed penny left behind, I profoundly regret my failure to adhere to Mick's advice about his cousin Eli.

CHAPTER 2

"Be a pal and do me a real solid."

"**AL, BE A PAL** and do me a real solid," says Mick's cousin, Eli Ativa.

I look up and Mick's cousin Eli's standing before me, as I am hurriedly packing my bag for a closing.

The mess I now find myself in began days ago at the start of a very busy, hectic Friday, when I had a major closing, which I know would run for much of the day and likely into the evening, if not past midnight. This is the kind of closing I dread, as so much time often gets wasted with arguing over asinine, mostly far-fetched, obscure theoretical issues that the lender's attorneys would inevitably raise at the eleventh hour and drive everyone nuts. And none of those issues did ever amount to anything.

As I am stressing over whether I had everything I needed, there's Eli in front of me with a shit-eating grin on his face.

I am puzzled by his presence. "Oh, hi Eli. Isn't Francesca out there?"

"Yeah, she's there," Eli says.

I say, "Eli, excuse me for a second."

I call out, "Francesca?"

"Yes, Al," my top-notch assistant, and cousin, Francesca responds.

"Grab a seat, Eli," I say to Eli, then say to Francesca, "Please come in here."

"Sure," she says. She comes into my office, sees Eli and says, "How the hell did you sneak in here, Eli?"

"Walked in."

Francesca says, "Didn't you see me sitting at my desk?"

"Yeah, but you were obviously concentrating on something and I didn't want to disturb you."

Francesca says, "You're a lawyer. I assume you don't expect anyone, not even another lawyer, for that matter, to just walk in on you without first letting your secretary know in order to be announced."

"Franny, besides the fact I don't have a secretary or a real office, as you well know, it's not like I'm a stranger or anything. You guys know me forever. Shoot, Al and I go back to when we are kids."

I say, "Okay, okay, *basta*, that's enough. But, Eli, please don't ever again barge in here without first letting Francesca know you're here. You don't know if I have a client in here or if I'm on a conference call, or up to what have you—and can't be disturbed."

"Shit, all right, Al. Don't understand why you have to get so uptight and by-the-book with me all of a sudden. Take a chill pill and give me a break."

Francesca says, "Al, you better get out of here quick. Peg O'Brien, the title closer, just called. She's at the closing already and needs to go over some title issues with you so she can get back to her clearance officer."

"I'm just about ready to go out. Call Peg back and have her email me her issues, and I'll email her back while I'm on my way there on the subway."

"Sure thing, Al."

Eli says nothing, just quietly waves goodbye to Francesca, who is several months pregnant with her first child. During that Gilbert child support matter, Mick devised various strategies to thwart the dirty tricks we were sure Gilbert would pull against Mary and me and my team. As a precaution against Gilbert's or his goons' going after Francesca, Mick had Francesca's husband Jimmy escort her to and from work every day. I figure this newfound togetherness resulted in push-comes-to-shove and everyone is now happily looking forward to the arrival of Francesca's and Jimmy's first born. Me? I do not know how I will survive while Francesca is out on maternity leave, and I'm deeply concerned that she may choose to be a stay-at-home mom. But that's my cousin's and her husband's decision. I recognize, and reluctantly accept, that the baby's best interest trumps me and my law practice. There are plenty of legal assistants—though those with Francesca's skills are scarce—and there will only be one first child for Francesca and Jimmy.

"Okay, Eli, I am running out for this mega closing. I'm late already. Please be quick. What's up?"

"Al, I need you to be a pal and do me a solid."

"And what may this so-called solid be? And couldn't it wait until some other time? You just heard I'm already running late."

"This is only going to take a minute of your time, Al."

Heard that before, as I recall.

"Okay, quick, please, what is it?" I ask.

"Okay, thanks. My opposition papers on this personal injury matter I'm handling have to be filed today or the motion for summary judgment brought by the plaintiff will be granted on default and my client screwed."

"You had to have been well aware of that."

"Of course, I am well versed in the court rules."

"And so, I know you were not sick or otherwise incapacitated these last few months. I also know that you have a very limited practice. So, what could have prevented you from beating the clock?"

"Al, don't lecture me. You're starting to sound like Mickie."

Mickie. Eli is the only person on earth who refers to Mick as Mickie, and it drives Mick nuts whenever Eli calls him that. Eli ignores Mick's threats, and I suspect relishes Mick's displeasure. It's just Eli being Eli.

"Eli, I just know it. You've been wasting your time with those foolish, frivolous interests of yours, ignoring pressing client matters which should take priority."

"Screw you, Al, I love basketball and old-school soul and R&B music. They're some of the few things that make this life worth living."

That expression Eli stole from Mick. Nevertheless, Mick's position is vehement that Eli's priorities are cockeyed and misplaced.

"Besides, a matter of civic importance has been taking up much of my time."

"Okay, Eli, I don't have the time. I have to go. What do you need from me?"

"I need to borrow your computer. Mine broke down last night and I need yours to do these papers that have to be filed electronically with the court by end of business today."

"The public library, even the law library at Brooklyn Law School, our alma mater, has computers you can use. I have lots of confidential personal and client stuff on my computer."

"So many different people use those public machines that they break down easily and I don't think they're secure. I know Julius maintains your system and trust that your machine is secure and will work. And if I run into an issue, I can get Julius to fix it."

Julius Ortiz is Mick's computer guy, who quite ably assists me as well.

"I don't think Francesca will want you in her hair today."

"I need to take it to my office and work on it there. I have all my files there."

"Your office? You mean D'Amato's Café on Court Street?"

"Yeah. Their Wi-Fi system is secure."

Just then, Francesca yells out, "Al, Peg just called again. She says everyone's there and they're all bitching about your not being there yet. You have to get going."

"Damn it, Eli. Take the friggin' machine. Just make sure you secure it and get it back here later today in the same condition it's in now. And do not screw around with any of my files. Create a separate file folder for your work. You should be able to easily figure out how to get online to access the court's website to file your papers. You have any questions, call Francesca or Julius.

"Take this and go."

I hand Eli my computer bag into which I had loaded my laptop computer, its mouse, power cord, and security lock. Eli takes the bag and off he goes with a smile and a wave.

I then grab my closing bag and dash out of my office. What I should have done was go and have my head examined.

CHAPTER 3

"Looks like every single one of your accounts has been cleaned out."

"Hello, Mr. Forte?"

"Yes, who's this?"

"Hi. It's Christine from St. Paul's. Is now a good time?"

"Oh, hi, Christine. I'm in the middle of a house closing, but there's a lull; so, I do have some time. What's up?"

"I just got a call from Mr. Scotto at the church's bank. He says you also bank there and that he tried to call you too. He says that your check from last week's collection bounced."

"Bounced? I didn't hear from him. I'm out of the office now and he probably called me at home or at the office and didn't try me on my cell. Okay, I'll call him as soon as I can. Thanks for letting me know."

"You're welcome, Mr. Forte. But what should I do with this past Sunday's check? Hold it until you talk to Mr. Scotto?"

"No, that shouldn't be necessary. I have plenty of money in my checking account. There must have been some error on the bank's part. Go ahead and deposit that check. Let me get back to this closing."

"Okay, thank you, Mr. Forte."

This is really strange. I couldn't imagine what went wrong. I go back to finish up the closing and call Tony Scotto as soon as I walk out of the seller's attorney's office.

His assistant, Karen, picks up his line.

"Hi, Karen, this is Al Forte. Is Tony available? I hear he's trying to reach me."

"Hi, Mr. Forte. I know that Mr. Scotto wants to talk to you, but he didn't get a chance to fill me in on the particulars. Unfortunately, a family emergency came up and he had to run out of here right away. I'll tell him that you called and have him call you in the morning."

"Just tell him that I called him back, but that I will call him as soon as I can tomorrow. I'll be tied up first thing in the morning with a series of hearings and will call him the first chance I get."

"I'll let him know. Thanks, and good night."

"Good night, Karen."

Although I know this bounced check business is because of some slipup on the bank's part, it still troubles me enough that I check my bank book balance, see that all written checks are duly noted on the check register, and confirm neither Theresa nor I had withdrawn any cash from the checking account. Satisfied, I put the issue out of my mind, but I decide, rather than call Tony Scotto, I will pay him a visit after my hearings. I need to stop by the bank to deposit the checks for my legal fees for last week's big closing and for today's house closing into my office's operating account in any event, and I would pass the bank on my way to the office after those hearings.

◆

"TONY, HEAR YOU trying to track me down."

"Yeah, Al. Francesca told me yesterday you were at a closing and then I had to run one of my kids to the doctor. My wife was tied up with her parents. You know they're in assisted living on the other side of Brooklyn.

"Anyway, I was notified that your check—for what? 40 bucks? —bounced and wanted to let you know right away. I didn't even get a chance to check your account myself and was going to have Karen do it when the call came in about my son."

"How's your boy doing, Tony?"

Ignoring me, Tony says, "So, first thing this morning, I have Karen check and she tells me that the account is zeroed out."

"What? Zeroed out? That's impossible. I checked my bank book last night and there's over ten thousand in that checking account."

"That's interesting, but the first question I asked was: If the checking account doesn't have enough money, you still have overdraft protection. So, why wasn't the check covered by the savings account that's supposed to fund your overdrafts?"

"Yeah, that's right." I acknowledge this as a matter of fact but am very confused about what I'm hearing.

"Well, we then discovered that your savings account and even your money market account are also zeroed out. While we're at it, we looked into your business accounts and are shocked to see that your business checking, savings and money market accounts now have zero balances as well."

"What?!"

"And, Al, that's not even the worst of it."

"How the hell can this possibly get worse?"

"Well, keep seated, because it looks like every single one of your accounts has been cleaned out."

"Wait, the only other accounts are my attorney escrow accounts. Those too?"

"Them too."

"Holy shit! We're talking about over a million dollars, may be close to two million!"

"That's right."

"How the fuck did this happen? Has to be some bank screwup."

"Well, we're investigating. These transfers happened via online banking."

"Wait. I rarely utilize online banking. I only use it if it's impossible to get to the bank. And you can be damn sure that I didn't authorize anyone else to do it. Theresa certainly didn't do it. She never uses online banking; like me, she prefers to bank face-to-face. Besides she's out of the country."

"Al, I believe you. But someone, somehow, used online banking for each and every one of your accounts and took out every single penny."

"What the fuck's going on! My head's spinning, just trying to get a handle on this bullshit. What the hell are you talking about, and how the fuck could it have happened, and how do we get this fixed? The bank must be culpable here."

"Well, listen Al, the full extent of this has only just now come to my attention, and we have started to make every effort to sort it all out. If we did screw up, I personally will make sure we do right by you. But if it was some criminal thing beyond our control, I honestly don't know what to tell you.

"In fact, I was instructed to inform you that you will not be dealing with me on this issue, but with our security folks."

"Listen, this must be fixed quick. While I'm certainly worried about my personal and business funds, I do not know where to begin with my just about shitting my pants about the escrowed monies. I have closings coming up and what am I going to tell my clients and the parties who entrusted their funds with me?"

"Well, do you have malpractice insurance?"

"Fuck you, malpractice! What the hell you talking about, Tony? You pinning this on me?"

"Al, Al, please calm down. I realize you're stressed. I'm just fishing for potential short-term solutions. No offense intended. Please, we go way back, Al."

"Sorry, Tony, this is just so upsetting. Sorry about what I just said."

"No sweat, Al. Your reaction is perfectly understandable. I don't know how I'd react if I were in your shoes.

"Anyway, like I said, the bank is drilling down to get to the bottom of this. I wrote out whom you'll be talking to about it. This guy Simmons says to give him and his people some time to sort it all out and for you to expect to hear from him tomorrow or the following day, this coming Monday at the latest.

"Regarding your personal money, I could front you up to ten thousand dollars without interest, on account of the circumstances. The same goes for your business checking account."

"That may not be necessary, but thanks. As I said, my main concern is the escrow monies. I have to figure out what I have to do. I probably need to notify the Client Protection Fund, and I am afraid to consider what will flow from that."

"Well, again, we're still sorting things out. So, you may want to sit tight until you and Simmons connect."

"Yeah. You're probably right.

"Okay, let me get back to the office and try to get some work done.

"Thanks, Tony."

"Good luck, Al."

I thought to myself, without a doubt, luck is what I'm definitely going to need.

CHAPTER 4

"There's no money there!"

As I walk into my office, I am greeted by a sobbing Francesca.

"Franny, what's the matter?" In professional matters, I address my cousin as Francesca; in personal matters, she's Fran or Franny.

"What the frig's the matter? You wanna know what's the matter? Do you? Well, I just got a call from my bank. When they tried to get my pay from the office account by direct deposit, there's no money there! And my monthly mortgage payment is by auto-pay from my checking account, and since my salary wasn't paid, there isn't enough to cover the mortgage payment. With the expenses preparing for the baby, we're really tight money-wise, and I was relying on my salary to cover most of this month's mortgage payment.

"What the fuck's going on, Al?"

"Oh, shit!" I think to myself.

"My God, I can't tell you how sorry I am about this screwed up situation, Franny. I'm just coming from Charter Bank, and somehow all my money's mysteriously been removed from all my accounts. It's an absolute mess, but Tony Scotto assures me the bank is actively working on getting to the bottom of it, and hopefully it'll all be straightened out within the next few days.

"Anyway, I will cover your salary with cash Theresa has stashed at the house."

"Well," Francesca says, "this explains why Mick sounded so pissed when he called earlier wanting to know when you'd be back. If I know Mick, you'll be facing him soon. Your rent check must have bounced too."

Sure enough, who should storm in at that very moment but my favorite cousin Mick. And he did not look happy at all.

"I wanna know what the fuck's goin' on here? Since when you start playin' basketball with your checks?" Mick is serious when it comes to collecting the money that is due him, even when it is due from someone as close to him as I am.

"Mick, I will make good on the rent once the bank gets to the bottom of a problem that just happened with my bank accounts."

"What the fuck you talkin' about? What's happenin' withcha accounts? Some kinda run on your bank? Can't be, 'em days are over. Charter Bank ain't no fly-by-night joint. What kinda jive you tryin' to run by me, cuz?"

"Right now, it's still a big mystery, Mick. All I know is that all of my accounts—personal, business, even escrow—were emptied out."

"*U' cazz!* That gotta be lots of dough you talkin' about. Your bank's legit, somethin' like you say ain't could happen. Just ain't possible."

"As I said, Mick, it's baffling to us all. Tony Scotto tells me the bank's security people are looking into it, and I'll hear from them in a matter of days."

"Yeah, I know Tony. I hadda kick his brother's ass once. But other than that prick, the rest of the family's all right. Even did some things with his father, a stand-up guy."

"Rest assured that the bank and I are taking this very seriously. Poor Franny's salary wasn't funded, and she can't make this month's mortgage payment. For myself, I haven't had a chance to consider the ramifications of this mess; you know, my bills that get auto-paid, checks I issued that are still outstanding—the whole thing. So, there's lots for me to catch up. In the short-term, Theresa has cash squirreled away in the house. And I'm carrying around checks for my fees for recent closings. I was going to deposit them today but didn't once this problem with my accounts came to light."

"Al, sign those checks over to me. Fran, you come and see me later. I'll give the checks to Cohen. He'll have your paycheck ready for you by time you pass by on your way home. He'll handle the deductions for FICA and the rest, as he usually does.

"Whatever's left over I'll hold 'til this fucked up mess's over, just in case it ain't fixed by the time Fran's next pay is due and there are other things that gotta get paid quick. I'll let the rent ride for the time bein'. And when we do settle up on the rent you owe me, you're gonna be coverin' the bounced check penalty Cohen makes me charge; that goes for late fees too. Doncha think I'm gonna make an exception and treat you special. Gotta make you an example for the deadbeats I gotta deal with every day."

"Fine. I appreciate your helping with Franny, and I agree with the rest. But I do expect it all to be sorted out and fixed tomorrow or in the next couple of days."

Mick huffs out of the office, surely disappointed that this kind of problem ever arose with me.

Whatever the underlying issue is, I am grateful that my wife Theresa is away for a while, touring Southeast Asia with an aunt and a couple of cousins. Due to technical and other restrictions, we'll be unable to communicate for much of her trip. Otherwise, there would have been hell to pay until this mess gets straightened out.

CHAPTER 5

"It will take us awhile to get to the bottom of this."

"SO FAR, BASED ON OUR very preliminary investigation, our initial conclusion is that we are not dealing with a situation where your accounts were raided by someone who hacked our systems."

Thus, begins the conversation between Mr. Henry Simmons, the chief cyber investigator for Charter Bank, and me on the Monday morning following my visit to the bank.

To this opening statement, I say, "Great. That's good news, right?"

"What do you mean by 'good news'?"

This question and particularly the tone in which it is spoken are troubling.

"Well, if my accounts weren't hacked, then some sort of computer glitch had to be the culprit. This would mean that the monies taken from my accounts did not leave the bank, and they can be simply returned to my accounts."

"Actually, you are mistaken."

"Mistaken? If there was no hacking, what else could have caused my accounts being emptied?"

"You or someone with your information used online banking and emptied each and every one of your accounts. Personal checking and savings. Business checking and savings.

Personal and business money market accounts. All of your escrow accounts."

"Wait, wait, wait. This is starting to sound like identity theft."

"Yes, that well may be the case. However, we and other financial institutions have recently had instances where other attorneys have, in fact, gone in and raided their own accounts and even their attorney escrow accounts. Those crooked lawyers sent the funds to untraceable offshore accounts and then claimed they were victims of identity theft and sought to recoup the stolen funds from the victimized banks. One such attorney in Oregon was convicted for doing that just last week."

"Wait! Hold on a second. You're not saying that I pulled some kind of scam and stole my own monies and the monies I was holding in escrow, are you?"

"Well, we are not in a position to allege that presently. As I said, our investigation is still in its preliminary stages, and any conclusion would be premature."

"When did these online banking transactions happen?"

"The Saturday a week ago, starting at approximately 12:15 a.m."

"I assume it took quite a while for each account to be accessed and for each of the transfers to be done."

"Yes, it took over an hour."

"Well, I must have fallen asleep by 12:30, fifteen minutes after you say the transfers started and was sound asleep well before the last one happened. Also, my computer was with me in the bedroom, turned off. I got back late from an all-day closing, stopped by the office at around 9 that Friday night to pick up mail and my computer so I could catch up on emails and work during the weekend, and did not turn my computer on until sometime after 10 a.m. Saturday morning."

Simmons says, "Anyone with you?"

"No, I was home alone. My wife's away in Asia."

"What you say is all fine and good and will be noted for the record, but the investigation will proceed, and the chips will fall where they may."

"What you are saying to me is that you won't be taking my word for it."

"That is correct."

I say, "Listen, Mr. Simmons, my reputation is spotless. I have banked with Charter Bank over twenty years. There's never been an instance of my issuing even one check that bounced or any of my accounts—personal, business or escrow—ever being overdrawn. Talk to Tony Scotto. We go back to grammar school."

"Yes, Mr. Forte, Mr. Scotto has vehemently vouched for you. However, given these other instances of false identity theft claims, or self-executed identity thefts, we are now required to thoroughly verify the validity of any such claims. In fact, this has become such a serious concern that, given our federal charter, the Federal Bureau of Investigation is as a matter of course notified of these instances and is often brought in to assist in our investigation and at times even launches its own independent investigation."

"The FBI? You've got to be kidding."

"Let me blunt, sir." His switch to "sir" from "Mr. Forte" was disconcerting and stomach-churning.

"Blunt? Blunt about what?"

"We are aware of your connections with known members of organized crime."

"What the hell could you possibly be referring to?"

"Is not Mr. Michelangelo, or Mick, Forte a cousin of yours?"

"Mick? Yes, of course, sure, he's my cousin. Yeah, but he's cleaned up his act."

"He does have a record and has been a person of interest on numerous criminal matters in the past. We know that he served a one-year prison sentence for assaulting someone said to be a borrower of his suspected loan shark operation."

"Please. My cousin is now as clean as can be. In any event, we never had mutual business connections."

"Is he not your present landlord? This office is in property of his, right?"

"Well, yes, he does own this property, but I do pay market rent, and my lease terms are arms-length. I have no sweetheart deal here."

"Well, I mention that only so you are fully aware of what's transpiring. Mr. Scotto indicated that he—and you as well—thought this would be resolved in a matter of days. I must inform you that it will take us awhile to conclude our investigation. And that is the case whether the FBI joins our investigation or conducts its own investigation. In the interim, Charter Bank is giving you the benefit of the doubt, which is why we are being so upfront with you."

He adds that based on its preliminary finding, the bank will not honor the offer of assistance Scotto said he would extend to me the other day. He also says that while federal law provides generous protection for claimed unauthorized withdrawal of funds from personal accounts, such protection will not be afforded to me pending the completion of the bank's investigation. Simmons also tells me that until the investigation is concluded my Charter Bank credit card and associated cash advance facility will be suspended.

Simmons's last words to me are a "friendly warning" to keep away from the bank and Tony Scotto and to let the investigation run its course. Simmons also issues what he refers to as "friendly advice" to cooperate fully with the investigation and to carefully consider not doing anything that would indicate guilt by, for example, retaining counsel.

"Thanks a lot" is what I say to Simmons as he leaves my office; "thanks for nothing" is what I think.

Once Simmons exits my office, the first thing I do is pick up the phone and call Richie Abbatello, Mick's criminal defense attorney and the attorney who got me out of jail when I was arrested during the Gilbert child support matter. Richie is the only one of Mick's friends growing up who became a lawyer. His impressive criminal defense practice is built on ties to guys from the old neighborhood. He's one shrewd, diligent, tough—and honest—lawyer, a good attorney to have when the possibility of jail is staring you in the face.

CHAPTER 6

"We're going to need Julius's assistance."

"WE'RE GOING TO NEED Julius's assistance with this." So said Richie Abbatello during our meeting the afternoon following my morning meeting with Simmons.

I was lucky that Richie had an early day in court and could stop by to see me in the early afternoon.

While he eats the lunch Francesca ordered for him, I bring him up to date with what had happened with my accounts and with what Charter Bank's chief cyber investigator had to say.

I ask Richie how worried should I be about this situation.

"As this guy told you, the investigation is just in its preliminary stages. But I am worried about the possibility that they will try to pin this on you. I've had some experience in this area, and unless there is clear evidence that you had nothing to do with it, they will go after you, even if just to buy time before they need to pony up—if, in truth, they do have an obligation to pony up at the end of the day.

"Now, before we go any further, there is something I need to know."

"You want to know if I'm pulling a fast one on the bank?"

"Bingo, you're right. I know the answer is no, but I have to ask."

"The answer is: of course, no."

"Sorry for having to ask, but I still had to hear directly from you what you had to say about that, to get it out of the way."

"And this guy Simmons told me the transfers happened at 12:15 in the morning, on a night when I had my computer with me at home in my bedroom turned off. I must have fallen asleep by 12:30, so there was no way that I could have done those transactions."

"Anyone home with you?"

"No. Theresa's away."

"So the fact that your computer was not in use and you were asleep is not going to help, because you're the only person who could testify to that. But even if we could convince Charter Bank, and anyone else who's interested, that you did not do those online banking transactions, someone must have somehow gotten your passwords and log-in information, and executed those transfers using some other computer. We'll have to establish that that person or persons who executed the transfers were not acting on your behalf, nor acting with your knowledge or consent. We'd also have to show that those transactions were not a result of serious carelessness on your part.

"So, this is how I think we should proceed. We'll do our own investigation, to get to the bottom of who's behind what happened and how it was accomplished, and bring what we learn to Charter Bank's attention ASAP. Want to cut them off at the pass before they start to point fingers at you. Among other things, once you become a suspect, even if you're totally innocent, your reputation goes down the toilet and it'll take immense effort—and luck—to get vindicated. And when something like this happens to a practicing attorney, your practice is impaired, sometimes even doomed, and it's not easy to get it back on track."

"So, specifically what are our first steps?"

"First, we're going to need Julius's assistance with this."

◆

MICK FIRST MET Julius Ortiz, his computer guy, through his friend Matt Smith. Julius is Matt's wife's nephew.

Mick told me once how he hooked up with Julius. He said, "Outa the blue, Matt calls me one night; he'd just moved to St. Louis. Tells me his wife's nephew, Julius, was picked up by the cops durin' one of 'em stop and frisk things. Matt said Julius ain't all that clear, but he used his one phone call to call Matt for help and Matt called me, 'cause he knew I'd do anythin' to help him. I get hold of Richie and end up drivin' him to the place they're holdin' Julius, 'cause Richie's car's in the shop. We're lucky a cop buddy of mine's at the desk and he cuts it to the quick. He saw that Julius was brought in 'cause he ain't got no ID on him, as if there's a law that says the cops can throw you in the can if you ain't got no ID. Anyways, we're outa there in no time, and on the way to Julius's place I find out he's a self-taught computer guy but with no real job, strugglin' to get by makin' mostly nickels and dimes helpin' friends or others, mostly moochers, 'cause he ain't got one of 'em pieces of papers that's supposed to mean somethin', but don't mean shit if you ask me.

"I know I need a better computer set-up, so I tell Julius to come see me. He comes by and we talk. I tell him what I need, he tells me what else I need, like a public Wi-Fi network for each of my buildin's to keep my tenants happy. He does his thing and does a very good job for me. I pay him good for that work and hire him to come back on a regular basis to train my staff and take care of my system, and then I hook him up with other folks I know who need computer help, includin' Richie and you, Al. And Julius now's got hisself plenty of work; he's real busy and on his feet moneywise.

"He runs his operation from space in my office and even moved into one of my buildin's. This way I keep an eye on him for Matt the last few years of his life, since Matt took off for St. Louis to beat his addiction by gettin' away from certain places and certain fellas here in Brooklyn. Now, I do it for Matt's brother Smitty who lives in Harlem. After Matt died, his wife asked Smitty to look out for her nephew, since Smitty's the closest 'family' she and Julius got in these parts. Besides, me, of course."

Matt's brother Smitty is Bill Smith, a retired career veteran and currently a process server and jack of all trades at Adler & Stillman, the law firm that represented Gordon Gilbert in that child support case. Smitty was a great help and played a significant role assisting us to prevail in that case.

◆

RICHIE SAYS, "This involves a lot of complicated, technical stuff. We're going to need Julius's expertise with this shit as it's above our heads. My hope is that Julius will be able to somehow get to the bottom of what happened to your accounts quickly. He's one sharp dude. If he's able to sort it out, we present his findings to Charter Bank and get this worked out informally and quietly. This way we avoid false accusations, avoid court, and avoid FBI involvement. I will, nevertheless, contact the FBI agents we got to know in connection with that Gilbert thing. I'll talk to Agents Adams or Zachs and hopefully that will help to keep that agency at bay while we do our own thing trying to figure this out."

"Money's a problem, you know. How am I going to pay you, even pay Julius?"

"In the short-term, that isn't an issue. Eventually, I'll need to get paid and so will Julius. I assume Mick knows all about this and will step up to the plate, like he always does, and give you a hand."

"Well, yes, Mick is aware of some of this. However, I have not yet informed him about this morning's conversation with Simmons.

"Luckily, I had undeposited checks from closings which I signed over to Mick and he got his accountant Cohen to pay Fran's salary from that. He agreed to let the rent ride in case this mess goes on unresolved longer than we think. Until my chat with Simmons, I assumed this would be rectified in a matter of days. Now that I know that's not realistic, I don't know what I'm going to do after I exhaust the little cash I have at home. The other funds we have are in retirement accounts that can't be touched without incurring penalties and some stock holdings that are in Theresa's name, and would result in capital gains if they're sold. Theresa also has her own retirement accounts and some investment accounts and hell would have to freeze over before she'd allow any of that money to be touched for anything other than funding our retirement. I just may have no choice but to look to Mick for funding until this is resolved."

Richie says, "Let's see if he and Julius can get over here right away, so we can get our investigation off the ground quick.

"You call them. In the meanwhile, there are some calls I need to make."

I call over to Mick's office. Luckily, both he and Julius are there and available to get to my office within the hour.

CHAPTER 7

"Light every ... candle in sight."

"**Why the fuck you** botherin' Richie and Julius with this bullshit with the bank? Ain't you talked to Scotto, and the bank inspector or whoever you're supposed to talk to by now and have this whole *budell* fixed and all your money back where it all belongs?"

Those were Mick's words in lieu of a hello or other greeting.

Richie and I update Mick and inform Julius of what's transpired.

Mick says, "Shit, youse attorneys sure do have a license to steal. I ain't never even thought to pull a fast one like those crooked lawyers done. Empty my accounts and then cry about my identity being stolen and expect the bank to pony it all up. Nice way to double your money. And meanwhile, all this stolen loot's sittin' in some secret account on the beach on the Caribbean. Crap, I still got lots to learn. That's what I get for not goin' to law school."

Richie says, "Come on, Mick. Let's get serious. We have a big problem here.

"And it's even worse than even Al knows. While we were waiting for you and Julius to come over, I called my good friend, Tony Scotto, and he called me back on my cell using probably the only public phone booth still on Court Street, the one at that candy store across the street from Tony's bank.

"Tony let me know a couple of important items that that guy Simmons must have intentionally failed to mention to Al earlier today. So, Al is also hearing this for the first time.

"First, Tony says that even if the identity theft happened through no criminality on Al's part, there's a good chance the bank will seek to exculpate, excuse, in other words—sorry for the lawyer language, Mick—the bank from having to make Al whole to any extent, based on an allegation that the whole mess is due to negligence on Al's part. They'll claim he failed to protect his password or pin and to prevent unauthorized access to his computer."

I say, "I don't know how they could possibly substantiate that."

Richie says, "We'll see. And it just might be a *res ipsa loquitur* thing. Mick and Julius, that's a Latin legal expression that means 'the thing speaks for itself.' As applied to Al's situation, they'd say that negligence on Al's part is the only logical explanation for how someone could have gotten the information necessary to do those online banking transactions.

"But let me move on. Second, there's one factor that distinguishes Al's case from the other attorneys, besides the fact that Al's no crook and is as honest as they come. In those other cases the computers used to do the thefts were not the thieving attorneys' computers. In Al's case, the bank investigators say that all signs indicate that Al's own computer was used to make the withdrawals. So, unless we can show that someone else got to Al's computer, criminal charges are likely to be brought."

I say, "Richie, again, how the hell is that possible. As I told you and as I informed Simmons, the bank's investigator, at the time the bank said the thefts happened my computer was turned off and with me in my bedroom. And I was asleep for much of the period during which those transfers happened."

Richie says, "That's like a tree falling in the woods. No one, other than you, is privy to the truth. So, that fact depends on your credibility under the circumstances. And under these circumstances whoever the finders of truth may be will no doubt have a serious problem believing you, as your testimony is self-serving. Therefore, we must proceed as if that is not a fact, and somehow come up with solid facts that prove that you had nothing to do with those online banking transfers.

"Now, the negligence matter would be a civil suit. Money alone would be at issue there, for the bank would seek a ruling absolving it from having to pay Al any of the stolen funds. If criminal charges are brought, Al faces the possibility of jail if it's proven that he falsely claimed identity theft, when in fact he committed what can be called a self-executed or self-perpetrated identity theft by which he robbed those monies, some his own, but mostly third-party escrowed funds. In this case, Al'd be prosecuted in order to punish him for stealing and to deter anyone else from similarly attempting to fake an identity theft. If, by some horrendous luck, Al got convicted, that would absolve the bank from having to return any of that money."

Mick says, "Holy shit! How the fuck can somebody pull off somethin' like this? What you think, Julius?"

Julius says, "I've heard of these kinds of money-grab swindles. It's very involved and complicated and ain't easy to pull off. You need to first get your hands on very personal information and then have to know how to get around some very tight security protocols the banks now have in place. The trick is to convince the bank's computer that it's communicating with the customer. Besides account information and security passwords, the bank's level of security is lowered if it's interacting with what it recognizes as the customer's computer. That's the key."

"What do you mean that that's the key?" I ask.

Julius says, "A customer's username and password are the tip of the iceberg, when it comes to being able to get past a bank's so-called security goalie and being able to get to one's money. The username and password only unlock the first of many doors, so to speak. Let me explain it this way, if all you want to do is transact something that isn't substantial and something that you routinely do, the easier it is for that transaction to go through. If a transaction is something out of the ordinary—in terms of amount or what have you—then there are more hurdles imposed by the security goalie. Those hurdles get reduced if the computer being used is the one that the bank recognizes as its customer's computer. If it's something that's drastic, like here where accounts are being emptied, then another level of security hurdle is imposed. The most common security device is the texting of a special verification code to the customer's cell phone on file with the bank. The customer would then have to insert that code as part of the transaction in order for it to proceed.

"Now, I'm familiar with Charter Bank's security protocol. Back in the day, I was able to hack into it, and I know how the protocol has since been upgraded. So, the only way that someone other than you could have done what was done with your accounts is if that person had your user name and password, knew the account numbers of those bank accounts and did it at your computer with your cell phone nearby."

I say, "Shit, again, I didn't empty out those accounts, and there's no way in hell that anyone could have done it. At the time the bank says the theft happened, I was asleep and my computer next to me and turned off. Otherwise, my computer generally stays in the office, and my cell phone is always with me."

Julius says, "There are ways to replicate someone's computer and cell phone. It certainly isn't at all easy and very few people have the skills to do it. But the initial key is having access, and you'd be surprised how easily that can be accomplished."

Richie says, "Our job as attorneys is to get to the bottom of situations like this. And lots of times it requires pulling teeth. By this I mean we must push and push until we have exhausted all possibilities. Now, I heard you say that your computer almost never leaves your office and that your cell phone is always with you. I must ask: Are you sure? Has anyone ever broken into your office."

I say, "The answer to that is no. Remember we installed the most advanced security system when we were dealing with that Gilbert matter."

Mick says, "He's right about the security system. But you activate it every time nobody's in the office?"

"We do at the end of every work day and when I leave here after working on a weekend."

"But if you or Francesca are here alone and run out for coffee or somethin', the system's on?"

"No, we wouldn't turn it on if either of us leave during the day, knowing we'll return right away."

Julius says, "Well, that opens the possibility of access."

I say, "Of course, theoretically, you're right, but we do have these incredibly sophisticated locks that are definitely engaged when no one's here, even if it's just to run to the corner for a sandwich."

Julius says, "You or Franny ever see any indication of the lock being tampered with?'

"No."

Though she is at her desk, Francesca is clearly listening in to this conversation and comes over to the conference room and pipes in, "Al's right. And you can look at the lock. There's not a scratch or gouge or any sign that someone tried to pick it or mess with it in any way."

Mick says, "And Al's right about how tight that lock is. That too was done durin' the mess with that dick Gilbert."

Richie asks, "Okay about access here. But how about when you take your computer home?"

"We have the same alarm system and locks there. So, if someone broke in, Theresa or I would know, and it's only Theresa and I there and we rarely have guests at the house, but whenever we do, no one's ever wandered into my home office. And again, at the time the bank says the transfers happened, my computer was turned off and in the bedroom with me while I slept."

Richie says, "Let me push further. You sure you never let anyone use it, either here or at home or to take it somewhere and borrow it?"

Francesca says, "Yeah, don't you remember, Al. You let Eli use it that day you had an all-day closing out of the office. It was on the Friday before last. His computer was on the fritz, and he said he desperately needed one to do some court papers, and you let him use it. Did I hear you right that the bank says these transfers happened just past midnight of that same day?"

I fully remember this but dread having to reveal it for reasons that soon become apparent.

Mick's eyes bulge, his face turns crimson, and he jumps up looking like he's about to lunge across the table and throttle me. Richie and Julius and Francesca have a shocked and frightened look on their faces and shudder. Mick screams, "Eli? Eli! You fuckin' lent your computer to that asshole, that *u' cazz* whackadoodle cousin of mine, Eli? Ain't I told you three million four hundred thousand five hundred twenty-two friggin' times, if that *strunz* asks you for anythin', all you need is one very simple friggin' word. Two motherfuckin' letters. Means the same cocksuckin' thing in English, Italian and Spanish, and who knows what other stupid language. NO! NO! NO!—'til the *mang u' cazz* cows come home, no is all you hadda say to that *sfaccim* kook."

Richie says, "Mick, Mick, come on, calm down. Al's just helping a friend and brother lawyer. For goodness sake, your cousin!"

"Fuck you, Richie. I told this asshole *stunat* nice guy, to have *nient* to do with Eli, that lazy no-good piece of shit. I tell it like it is. Make no fuckin' difference that fucker shares some of the same blood with me. Don't know what the fuck happened to that screwball cousin of mine. He hadda hadda bumped his head or somethin'. He's got lots of loose screws. No, he's got bolts missin', he's so fucked up.

"Now, you Al, you fuckin' idiot, have hellava nerve to come cryin' to me for help. Fuck you! After I beg you so many friggin' times to stay away from that *pazz*, did my best to set you straight, you spit in my face, disrespect me and bend over backwards to help that lamebrain asshole. Here I am, helpin' you to make sure Franny's salary gets paid, lettin' my rent slide, and who you think is gonna bail you out when you're supposed to pony up alla that escrow money you ain't no longer got? You're gonna come to me, right? You think Eli'll bail you out or help you in any way? I should tell you to *va fa cul* and sell whatever you can pull out from your fat butt while you're at it."

Richie cuts in, "Listen, no question we have a mess on our hands. We need to put our heads together and fix it. Now, we don't know for a fact that this mess resulted from Eli's borrowing of Al's computer. But from the little that we do now know, that's definitely the first thing we need to check out.

"So, let's get hold of Eli. Get him in here so we can question him and find out if what happened to Al is because of something that occurred during the time Eli had Al's computer.

"I know Eli and doubt very much that he's a thief or dishonest in any way. You two, Mick and Al, you guys know him way better. Don't you agree that it's highly unlikely that he's the culprit here, that if what happened did happen while Eli borrowed Al's computer that someone else got to that computer?"

I say, "I think we can give Eli the benefit of the doubt."

Mick says, "Yeah, he's a screwball that ain't could be trusted, but he's not no crook."

Mick's cell phone then rings. Mick looks at who's calling and says, "I gotta take this. Be right back."

While Mick is out of the room to take that call, Richie says, "Scotto also told me that he went ballistic over the accusation Simmons made about your association with what he referred to as 'known members of organized crime,' namely, Mick. Scotto went as high up in the bank as he could, and Simmons was ordered that, unless he has or comes across hard indictment-worthy evidence to back up that accusation, he's not to raise it as an issue. With Mick's reputation in this neighborhood, Scotto warned his superiors that without solid evidence to back up any allegation against Mick, there'd be a customer revolt, a run on the branch, and Charter Bank would have no choice but to close the branch, which over the years has been one of its stellar branches. The PR flowing from that would be terrible for the bank. Scotto told his superiors that Charter Bank would be lucky if the branch didn't get burnt to the ground."

Mick returns and says, "I heard that last thing you just said and ain't could give two craps about that, but after listenin' to the rest of this shit, I gotta get somethin' offa my chest.

"Damn it, Al, this scumbag Simmons is givin' it to you right up the ass, in *cul*. You hear me? *Tu sienta me?* You ain't could let nobody, and I mean *nessun*, do that to you without no fight. You know you ain't done shit, nuttin' wrong at all. You gotta fight for your friggin' name, your goddamn honor and reputation. Your law license too.

"You ain't gonna just sit on your fat butt there and do nuttin' like you been doin'.

"It's me, that Simmons's ass wudda been grass. You, you a lawyer, you ain't could fight that way. You fight with words and paper, in court. I fight with fists in the street. Whatever the fuck the way you fight, is the way you gotta fight and just don't sit there doin' *u' cazz* while that asshole's reamin' you real good. You gotta make sure he knows you ain't takin' no shit from him and this motherfuckin' Charter Bank. Sometimes you gotta make sure they know you're ready to go toe-to-toe with 'em."

Richie says, "Mick, I know where you're coming from, but it's too soon to make this as adversarial as you suggest. That may force the bank to take a position that it wouldn't otherwise take to Al's detriment. And sure, perhaps Al could have been more assertive in setting this guy straight. But the time to fight like you say is not here yet."

Mick says, "Fuck you, Richie. I ain't could agree with you less. But it's Al's mess and you're his lawyer. If nice and

easy is the way Al and you think it should go, youse makin'
a big mistake.

"But, I said my piece. Youse do what youse think is best,
but don't come cryin' to me later about how youse got fucked
by waitin' too long to fight back.

"And even if youse're right, Richie, Al hadda hadda put
that fucker in his place. Let that asshole know upfront Al
ain't gonna put up with any of the shit that that scumbag's
shovelin'. Al shudda been pissed and let this Simmons know
it loud and clear, then and there. So he knows who and
what he's dealin' with. Al don't want that guy thinkin' he
ain't gonna have no battle royal if he thinks he could get
away with callin' Al and me a crook or Al careless. Shit, 'em
fightin' words and ain't could be said by nobody without no
proof behind 'em. You know that fuck's only guessin' and's
tryin' to pin this on Al to get the lousy bank off the hook.

"We're fightin' whoever's behind this—and Charter Bank
too, if it ain't change its tune. And we gotta find that *sfaccim
e med* Eli pronto, so we can figure out if this mess happened
when he had Al's computer. 'Cause if it ain't that, then we
gotta chase some needle in some huge friggin' haystack, and
there ain't no bookie who's gonna give youse no odds that
Al ain't gonna be fucked if that's what we're dealin' with.

"Friends, time's a-wastin'."

Francesca stuck her head in and says, "I tried to get hold
of Eli, but he didn't pick up his cell or home phone and hasn't
responded yet to the messages I left on those phones. And I
am still waiting for him to reply to the email and text I sent
him. Told him he needs to get in touch with Al pronto."

Richie says, "Thanks for being on the ball, Francesca."

Mick says, "Yeah, wish your fuckin' boss was on top of things as good as you, Franny."

Richie says, "Come on, cut it out, Mick.

"To get back on track, Al, once you hear back from Eli, get him here and we'll grill him and hopefully get to the bottom of this hell of a mystery and be in a position to fix it.

"I too hope this mess resulted from something that occurred while Eli had Al's computer. That should narrow down what we need to do to resolve it. If that's proves not to be the case, like Mick says, who the fuck knows who we have to chase and what we need to do."

Mick concludes the meeting by glaring at me straight in the eye and saying, "I don't give a shit about what Richie just said about bein' nice-nice, if Eli's got anythin' to do with this, you'd better get your ass to church and light every fuckin' candle in sight."

CHAPTER 8

Feeling terrible.

"JUST WAIT 'TIL I GET MY hands on that fuckin' Eli. Now, that screwball's over an hour late." Mick is getting increasingly agitated at unpunctual Eli.

The day after Mick, Julius, Richie and I meet, Francesca manages to track Eli down. She had called Jenny at D'Amato's, and asked Jenny to call her as soon as Eli came to "his office."

Jenny, knowing Eli as well as anyone, calls Francesca as soon as Eli waltzes in and walks the phone over to Eli, so he's forced to take Francesca's call.

"Eli, I've left messages for you all over. How come you never got back to me?"

"Oh, hi Franny, I've been running around nuts and I'm just now coming up for some air."

"Listen. Al has something very important to discuss with you. Needs to see you ASAP."

"Okay, let's see. I can come by the day after tomorrow."

"No, Eli. Al says it's urgent and imperative that you and he meet today."

"Franny, with all I've got going, I just can't do it on a moment's notice."

"You're something, Eli. You bother Al as he is rushing to a closing, after you sat on your client's case for who knows how long. He's got to do you a 'solid' on the spot, entrust you with his computer, and now he says he's got something important to discuss with you and you say it's impossible to accommodate him? Come on, get real."

"Okay, you're right, Franny. I'll come today, but it won't be 'til five."

"Fine. I'll tell Al you'll be here at five."

"I will be there sometime around five."

"Eli, be here at five. If you can't make it by five, then give Al the courtesy of a call. I know your folks taught you some manners."

"Franny, you need to have more respect for your elders."

"Eli, as far as you're concerned, I'll do just that once you grow up some."

"Listen. I have to go. See you around five. Bye."

All Francesca can do is shake her head.

I'm out of the office, but Francesca knows that five that afternoon is good for me. She calls Mick, Julius and Richie to see if any of them could join me and Eli. Mick says he could, but Julius and Richie both have conflicts and can't make it. We had previously agreed that this initial meeting with Eli was critical and would happen as long as at least one of us could meet with him.

Five comes and goes. Mick is becoming more and more irritated. Blowing off some steam first at Eli, then at me, does nothing to calm him.

At six, Mick says, "Send Franny home. I'm gonna have Paolo go to Eli's house and drag his ass here. If Eli ain't there, Paolo'll wait 'til that jackass shows. Theresa's outa town anyways, so it ain't like you gotta be home now to eat.

I'll order some food and we'll wait for that jerk all fuckin' night if that's what we gotta do."

Mick calls over to Mama Maria's and asks John to deliver a pizza to my office.

The pizza arrives in no time.

While we eat, Mick says, "Man, this is damn good pizza."

"You can say that again, Mick."

"Yeah, ain't nobody could make pizza like my man John."

"That's true, Mick. No question about it."

As we are finishing up our pizza, I think it's best to get Mick's mind off this mess for a while, mostly to avoid my being subjected to nonstop venting by Mick about Eli and about my stupidity. So, I ask him to tell me about how Paolo came to become part of his crew.

Mick says, "Let me tell you, Paolo's story's a funny one. Comes to me through Pedro. You know Pedro Ramos and me met in prison. He heard how I helped Malcolm get his grandma into one of my places and word got to me that his mother was about to be evicted and his crew on the outside ain't know shit about gettin' her into a decent place.

"So, like I done for Malcolm, I had my guys pack her up and move her to an empty apartment in one of my buildin's. And Pedro and I been tight from then on."

Richie Abbatello had told me about what he refers to as The Alliance that Mick forged with Malcolm and Pedro while in prison. Whether or not solidifying his safety in prison was Mick's motivation for the relationship, Mick didn't need to worry about protection, for there were many Mob associates there with him, and he grew up with a good number of correction officers and maintained good relations with them. But, as Richie saw it, it certainly did not hurt to have strong ties with the leaders of both the African-American and Latino prisoners. By establishing those new connections, Mick was like the prince of the prison.

And benefits ensued from The Alliance once Mick, Malcolm and Pedro were released from prison. Together they developed an informal job training program for released prisoners. Each had their own enterprises to run which needed loyal employees. They would match up candidates with jobs that seemed most suited for them among their separate respective operations, and their individual powers of persuasion helped their placements to succeed.

"Now, Paolo, as much as a thug he was, or thought he was, never was in no joint. He's from Pedro's neighborhood and was just a hanger-on in the beginnin'. Pedro would give him some small things to do, which Paolo usually screwed up. Pedro ain't could trust him to do things the right way. Then, Paolo was a lazy fuck-up.

"Anyways, Paolo and me first run into each other on a Saturday mornin' a few years back. I'm runnin' around, takin' care of this and that, rushin' to some appointment I ain't could remember now, when I'm drivin' down Bond Street hustlin' to make the light at Atlantic, when this absolute jerk in fronna me, in a Jeep with the top down no less, slows down to get on his cell and stops right as the light goes from green to yellow. If he'd only kept to the fuckin' speed he's goin' before the damn call, both of us cudda made that light.

"So, of course, this pisses the shit outa me," which did not surprise me in the least. "I just about standin' on the friggin' horn for a second or two—hey! I ain't appreciate that *disgraziat* smirk, cuz."

I had rolled my eyes at the "second or two" remark.

"Anyways, I yell at the fuck, 'Hey, asshole, if you ain't slowed down to take that call from the president, I ain't gonna be so damn fuckin' late for my appointment.'

"Well, the jerk, it's Paolo I'm talkin' about, turns around, puts an ugly puss on and yells, 'Pull over, you dipshit!' Now, he's gettin' me hot. There's this pump there with enough room for both of us, so we both pull over and jump outa our cars, glarin' at each other.

"He starts swearin' and screams at me: 'Who the fuck you think you are to disrespect me in this way?' Now, Paolo's maybe 22 then; he's about six feet and 225 or so, a serious body builder, with biceps bigger than my thighs.

"Me, you know I'm fifty-somethin' then, maybe five-foot six and 175, tough as can be, ain't no way nobody gonna hurt me, and nobody and nuttin' ain't gonna scare me. So, I says to him, 'Listen, muscle boy, you're the one who's disrespectin' me. Why the fuck you think the rules of the road say you ain't could talk on no phone and drive at the same time. You know, all your muscles are unda your neck. Your head's gotta be filled with rocks.'

"Well, he really goes off, says he's gonna do this, that and the other thing to me. Finally—now I'm still pissed, but I'm in control—I step back, put up my hands to slow his rantin' and says to him, 'Be quiet and listen to me for a sec. You ain't know me and so you ain't know who you dealin' with and what's gonna happen to you—and your loved ones, if you got any.' I hadda throw that little jab in there. 'So, if I'm you, I'd ain't dare mess with me 'cause I'd fuck you up real good. And if by some friggin' miracle you hurt me, you gonna learn a painful lesson you'll wish you ain't never got taught.'

"Paolo gives me a look of disgust and says, 'What you saying, bubba? You a wise guy from the mean streets? I know all about you has-been *goomba* good fellows. You're yesterday, I'm today and I run with Pedro Ramos's crew. I ain't afraid of you or yours and welcome you to bring it on, you old, fat fuckin' guinea, dago, greaseball!'

"His mention of Pedro gives me an idea. I pull out my cell and says to him, 'So you run with Pedro Ramos, right? Here, call him, use my phone, use up my minutes.' He don't wanna at first but takes my phone when he goes into his pocket and realizes his cell's still in his car.

"So, he dials and as he finishes dialin', starts starin' at my phone's screen. For, as I know (and knew all along), he sees '*Papi*' on the screen where the number he just punched in was. Then his face turns the color of burgundy right before my eyes, and he says into the phone, 'Yo!' then sorta stutters, 'a, no, no, this ain't no Mick. This is Paolo, *Señor* Ramos, you know, Paolo Ruiz from up the block. Yeah, sure, of course, *Señor*. Mick, you say, a, he must be right here. No. Juan ain't here. I don't know about that, *Señor*. Yeah, well something happened and this old guy and me got into it, and he was real nasty and called me out and all and…. Okay. Here he is.'

"He hands me the phone. He's shufflin' his feet and looks like he's about to stink up his bloomers.

"I take the phone and says, '*Buenos días, Papi!*'

"Pedro Ramos says, 'Mick, what's Paolo doing with your phone and what's happening between you two?'

"I tell him, 'This guy and me got into words after I yell at him for slowin' down to take a call and makin' me miss a light. Then he tries to tell me what he's gonna do to me, and I try to let him know who he's dealin' with. Then, he tells me he runs with you, and you and your boys're gonna kick my and my boys' asses—and so on, you know how it usually shakes out. So, I give him my phone and tell him to call you and here we are.'

"Pedro says, 'Mick, put your phone on speaker. I want Paolo there to hear what I have to say.'

"'He wants this on speaker,' I tell Paolo, as I hit the speaker button, and then tell Pedro, 'Okay, *Papi*, it's on speaker. Go ahead.'

"Pedro says, 'Paolo, what I have to say I want both you and my very good compadre there, Mick, to hear.' Paolo takes a deep swallow.

"'Paolo, Mick and I go way back. Both of us will fight to the very death to protect each other. You hear? Did you hear me, Paolo?'

"Paolo nods.

"I says, '*Papi* can't see you nod.'

"Paolo says, '*Sí, Señor.*'

"Pedro continues, 'Good. Mick and I were in the joint together. I was real wild and out of control then. You know me as a faithful family man now, but then I only gave a crap about myself—until I met up with Mick. In the joint, my junkie sister, the one I told you about who died from an overdose, visited me crying about our moms's getting evicted from her apartment. I was totally helpless, 'cause before the joint I lived here and there, had no money handy and no way to keep my moms from being thrown out on the street. I didn't know the man, only heard of his rep after he got tight with this brother that the blacks ran with in the joint. I heard that he helped this dude Malcolm's family. Didn't know what exactly he done, but—anyway—I was desperate and go to him, and Mick says, "Sure, I can help your mother." Truth is I didn't trust him. Why would this Italian gringo want to help me, a drug-dealing Rican? He says he can arrange for my moms to move, that he has people who will move her and her stuff and then we'd work out the details about rent later. I wanna know what's in it for him and he says, 'our future friendship.' He says, 'I've watched you and got a feelin' that we're *simpático* and am willin' to take this chance to test my intuition.' Anyways, he does it, and next thing I know my moms's besides herself with joy, living in a great apartment, living with lots of nice neighbors. And today, she's in her eighties, still in one of Mick's apartments with others her age and loving it. Mick and his people look after her and if she needs something at the store or a ride to the senior center, the doctor's or church, they're there for her, if I can't be.

"'So, if you, Paolo, a no-good, muscle-bound *maricón*, even think of touching my friend Mick, I will have you tortured horribly and if I should somehow be overtaken by mercy, kill you to make your misery come to an early end. But Mick don't need me to protect him. You're wrong to disregard his warning, for he himself will have no trouble kicking your ass up and down Atlantic Avenue there without breaking a sweat. And should you somehow get lucky and avoid that fate and even hurt him, his people will get to you and you will live to regret your encounter with him.

"'*Finalmente,* you lousy no-good *estúpido Puertorriqueño,* Paolo. You are never, ever to tell anyone that you have anything to do with me. You are not even allowed to tell anyone that you know me, unless you have my permission. And that permission must be in writing, signed by me before two witnesses and a notary. Are we *claro* about this, Paolo?'

"Paolo whispers into the phone that I put next to his mouth, '*Sí, Señor.*'

"'Let me say one more thing,' Pedro continued. 'I actually thought of sending you to Mick to learn an honest living from him. Remember I asked you before about Juan? Well, just this week, Juan, on my referral, started working for Mick. Is he working out, Mick?'

"'Sure is, *Papi.* I could use four others like him,' I tell Pedro.

"'Well, I am meeting with this other young man and his folks tomorrow after Mass, and if I have a favorable impression, I may be able to fill one of those spots by Monday. I could never send Paolo to you. He's nothing but a lazy bum. He gets his money selling his body to needy women. A Rican *gigoló.* A real piece of *mierda.*

"'And, by the way, Paolo, you'd better lay low with that fancy car of yours. Just ten minutes before this call, the repo man was on the block with his tow truck. So, you'd better pay up if you want to keep your pretty ride.

"'Now that we all understand each other, I and Mick have better things and better people to be concerned about, unless Mick wants to teach you a lesson you'll never forget. But I suspect he'd like to wrap up this meeting and move on.'"

"'That's right, *Papi, adiós*,' I say. I click my cell off and Paolo and I go our separate ways."

I say, "Wow, that's some story. But, wait, Paolo is now one of your guys. Even when we had that meeting here at my office with Gilbert and his attorney, Paolo was here with Malcolm's guy Vernon to back you up."

"I really ain't need 'em for backup. I cudda handled it on my own. But if you got a situation like that showdown meetin' with that dick Gilbert and his hotsy-totsy attorney, where things cudda got physical, it's best to have muscle there, even if just for show. That way you got a better chance that the other side'll back down. They don't wanna get hurt. If all you got are small tough guys like me, the other side might make the mistake that they could get physical and rough us up some. Then we'd gotta clean up the mess me and my other small tough guys wudda made of 'em. But like you know, we ain't needed Vernon and Paolo, 'cause we already had Gilbert by the balls and the law got there before things got messy.

"Anyways, Pedro and my double-teamin' of Paolo somehow did him some good. Banged some sense into Paolo's head and the next week he goes to Pedro and begs for another chance. Pedro tells him that he's gonna hafta prove he's willin' to learn and change his attitude and in time Paolo comes around. He learns some plumbin' and electricity, and I take him on as a handyman, and he now runs the maintenance crew for my places in Carroll Gardens. The guys on his crew and my tenants are very happy with him. And Pedro and me are glad things worked out for the kid, who looked like he was takin' an express to the joint."

Mick then looks at his watch, stares me in the eye and says, "Wait a motherfuckin' second, you think I ain't know what you doin'? You get me tellin' you this story so you ain't gotta hear me belly achin' about how pissed I'm at both you and that jackass Eli.

"Well, Mr. Smarty Pants, fuck you, 'cause I'm now even more ticked off at you and that whacked-out kook. I'm tired of havin' to solve problems that you create, especially if 'cause you ain't listened to somethin' I already told you a million times. And I don't know why I'm wastin' my and Paolo's time, when it's you who gotta get off your fat ass and clean up this mess of yours. Paolo and me are goin' home. You go chasin' after that asshole Eli. You gotta figure out if this *budell*'s 'cause of your lendin' your computer to that dope or if it's 'cause of somethin' else. Once you know what the story is, maybe I'll think about givin' you a hand. You know, why the fuck should I give a fuck about this, if you yourself ain't givin' no fuck about it?

"Good night, you lousy dipshit."

With that, Mick storms out of my office, leaving me behind feeling terrible.

CHAPTER 9

"They call it the head-banger."

As Mick storms out, I sit there stunned.

I think to myself: Poor Mick. Ever caring, always willing to help. He's expected to lead the charge while the rest of us just sit back and let him resolve our problems for us. I realize the frustration he must feel, and that he must feel taken advantage of by me.

This is not the case when he helps someone from the neighborhood. Those are truly needy folks who are overwhelmed by some problem, who do not know how to resolve it, who have no choice but to depend on Mick and his resourcefulness. They are helpless without him. Mick knows and accepts this, but he is compensated by the respect and gratefulness that those folks feel toward him.

With me and others like me, we step back and let, expect even, Mick to take the lead. After all, I'm busy, I have to attend to my clients and their legal matters. My clients are supposed to be my principal obligation as part of my professional responsibility. Mick will take over, take the lead, help me out. I can leave it to him, there's no need for me to lift a finger.

I feel terrible. I realize Mick's frustration and feelings of disrespect. He too has a multitude of responsibilities, he has businesses to run, tenants to keep comfortable, employees to keep gainfully engaged, those truly in need to help. He, like the rest of us, has a breaking point and can only do so much.

I'm more than capable of resolving my own problems. All I have to do is overcome my complacency, not permit my busy practice serve as a lame excuse that allows me, consciously or unconsciously, to leave everything in Mick's lap. I must be more proactive and lead the team, a team that I surely need to resolve this mess. Mick and his crew will certainly be part of that team, but like I had preached to Mick when we were arguing about his role in the Gilbert matter, I must call the shots in collaboration with him and the other team members.

I eventually get home about midnight, shower and fall right into a fitful sleep.

I call Mick first thing the following morning and apologize for not taking command of this mess of mine.

"Appreciate the call, Al. Ain't could be there all the time to wipe your ass, you know. You got yourself a real fuckin' problem, and that *strunz* Eli ain't gonna give two shits about nuttin' 'cept whatever tickles him. So, you gotta get off your big fat ass and do some shakin' and bakin' in the streets and track that asshole down. Otherwise, you just paddlin' yourself deeper and deeper up shits creek. Who the fuck knows? That *sfaccim* cudda wandered off and left your computer sittin' on the table at D'Amato's and anybody cudda walked in and swiped it."

"I did give Eli the locking device and told him to be sure to secure it on the table."

"Still, these computer hackers can do all sorts of shit once they get hold of a computer. You should see what Julius can do.

"If I'm you, I'd be shittin' in my pants with all the dough that's out the door. And fuck, you got those folks whose money you're holdin'—or used to hold—and you gotta worry too about 'em and the State or the Courts or whoever could take your law license away from you, 'cause you lost those folks' dough. 'Em folks're gonna be real pissed-and-a-half once they find this out. I'd think your bowels'd be in a friggin' uproar.

"Take this seriously 'cause you ain't could rely on *nessun* to get to the bottom of what the fuck happened. It's your dough, the dough of those who thought they can trust you, your license, your rep. You gotta fight to fix this. I'll help, but you gotta drive the bus. No ifs, ands or buts about it, Richie, Julius and me are gonna have your back, but you gotta take the lead and be there in front.

"Listen, I gotta go now and watch over some work bein' done at one of my places. Let me know later what's up. Then, me, you, Richie and Julius'll talk and decide on what's next to do."

I get to the office just after nine and Francesca is at her desk.

"Hey, good morning, Franny. Did you see Eli at D'Amato's when you went there for your coffee?"

"No, Al. Too early for him, but I did run into his wife Lucy. She said she emailed us both last night. Wait, here it is. 6:15, right after I left. You see it?"

"No. I turned off my machine before six last night. Haven't turned it on yet and didn't even check my phone for emails.

"What she say?"

"She said Eli forgot that he had a game last night. The Red Hook team he plays with had a tournament game against the team from the Gowanus Houses. It was supposed to be played this past weekend, but was cancelled because of a power failure. Lucy said Eli forgot it was rescheduled for last night."

"That fuck stood up Mick and me to play a game of basketball?"

"Apparently so. She was rushing to work but said everybody in the neighborhood's talking about the game. Said Jenny and Junior were there too. They didn't say anything to me about the game, but they were busy handling their morning rush."

"Okay, listen, I don't have anything pressing this morning. I'm going to D'Amato's to see if I can catch Eli there. I have to take the initiative about this mess with my accounts. Mick got pissed at me for expecting him to take the lead."

"He's right you know. As helpful as he always is, he doesn't like to be taken advantage of."

"Tell me something I don't already know."

Eli is not at D'Amato's Café when I arrive there just past ten. Jenny and Junior are taking a load off their feet now that things have settled down some, and I go over to talk to them.

"Hey, Al," Jenny greets me. "You should have seen your cousin on the court last night."

"Yep," says Junior, "he played some game. Led the Red Hook team to quite a victory over Gowanus."

I say, "Eli is not my cousin."

"What are you talking about, Al?" Jenny says. "He's Mick's cousin too, ain't he?"

"Yes, he is Mick's cousin, but Mrs. Ativa is Mrs. Forte's sister. My dad and Mick's dad are brothers."

Junior says, "Never knew that, and all these years thought you three were cousins."

"Anyway, Eli come by yet?" I ask.

Jenny says, "That pain ain't yet arrived. My guess is he's still in bed, tuckered out from all of his picking and rolling."

I call Eli's home phone and cell and leave voice messages on both to call me ASAP. I also email and text him to say the same thing. I call Francesca and direct her to follow up via all media periodically and to even call Lucy and let her know that it's absolutely critical that Eli and I connect. That Mick wants to talk with him too. Letting Lucy know Mick's also anxious to talk to Eli will heighten the urgency.

One of Eli's loves is playing basketball. He possesses amazing skills for someone his age and size. He's barely five foot six and is pudgy, weighs about 165. But he could sure maneuver on the basketball court, knows how to handle a basketball, and shoots with stunning accuracy. And he is even reputed to be able to dunk, although I don't know of anyone who's actually seen him do it. (When I asked Eli about this, he said that would be showing off, so he doesn't dunk in order not to be perceived as a ringer by his opponents.) He would play as often as he could, but no longer enjoys playing with folks his own age. So, via his contacts at the local Y, he has hooked up with some fellows from the Red Hook public housing project to form a team. That team then began to consistently win the annual Y tournaments, largely led by Eli's superlative play.

"Well, you missed quite a game last night, Al," Jenny says. "This dope, Dexter on the Gowanus team, tries to get Eli's goat. He calls Eli 'White-tay' and 'Pillsbury dough-daddy' to his face. Luckily, Shaquan, the Red Hook captain, pulls Eli aside and tells him to keep his cool and let his play do the talking. And he tells Eli to stick to mostly defense and to ball-handling on the offensive end. Says to Eli to leave scoring to the others unless he's wide open. I'm guessing Shaquan wants to make sure the other guys have a chance to contribute. Otherwise, Eli'd dominate."

Junior cuts in, "So, Red Hook proceeds to whip Gowanus's butts but good. Eli's feeding his teammates and picking and rolling, giving and going, back dooring and alley-ooping Gowanus to shame. You should of seen him threading the needle with his precision passes. He must of had ten assists in the first ten minutes. On D, Eli has four steals, three intercepted passes and four rebounds within the same time."

Jenny then takes her turn, "Red Hook's ahead by eleven baskets to zip, when that guy Dexter chucks a clunker from way out. The Gowanus guys crash the boards, but the Red Hook guys box them out nicely and Shaquan easily grabs the rebound. Eli breaks down court and Shaquan makes a perfect lob to him. Eli has strides over the closest Gowanus guy, happens to be that dope Dexter. We all could see Eli's eyes brighten up and him break into a huge smile."

Junior says, "You should of seen it. When Eli reaches the key, instead of driving to the hole, he jumps straight up and spins around. At the halfway point, that guy Dexter's a coupla strides behind him, charging like a maniac, just as Eli, now with his back to the basket but facing this Dexter, raises the ball overhead and rams that sucker into Dexter's fat head.

I couldn't believe it. The most amazing thing I ever seen. That ball arcs toward the hoop and the fuckin' thing goes in—not only without any backboard or rim, but also without any swish of the net. An unbelievable, perfect basket! Those of us seen Eli play call that shot one of his 'head-bangers'."

Jenny then says, "As you could well imagine, friggin' pandemonium breaks loose. Everybody's whooping and hollering like hell. And while us spectators are having the time of our lives, the director of the Y's there, and he's totally pissed."

Back to Junior, "That guy goes after Eli, bitching how could someone Eli's age and maturity conduct himself in such an unsportspersonlike manner, set such a terrible example, ain't he understand that he could of incited a riot.

"We find out later that Eli's suspended from the Y."

I say, "That's really something." Now wanting to steer the conversation to why I am sitting there and not at my desk in the first place, I say, "So, Jenny, what time does Eli usually arrive?"

Jenny says, "Eli doesn't exactly keep regular hours."

"Yeah, but your address is what's on his business card as the address for his law office."

Jenny says, "Eli, he comes here just about every day, and when he does, is here sometimes for an hour or so, sometimes longer. He took over that table over there in the corner. When he first started coming here, if there are folks there, he tells them it's reserved for him. After some folks gave him some lip, he started putting that sign that says 'Reserved' there; folks now stay away, and regulars know not even to go close to his table."

◆

ELI IS SO BRIGHT, he had no trouble getting high scores on the LSATs. He did not even do any prep work for the exam. He didn't go to a prep class or even buy a book with sample questions and do the drills to get familiar with the exam and the kinds of materials it tested—and it is an extraordinarily difficult exam with challenging logic questions and sophisticated math problems. I could not imagine how anyone could just walk in off the street and do well on that exam, no matter how bright and how accomplished scholastically. After much prep and practice, I did all right, but Eli scored higher than I did, as he consistently did on standardized exams.

It was a different story when it came to performance in class. In law school, my hard work paid off and I made law review. Eli just barely got by, mostly passing by the skin of his teeth.

His lack of effort did not mean he did not learn the law. One day I'm in the library, grappling with the conclusion of my law review article about a U.S. Supreme Court case on state aid to parochial schools. Eli sees me and stops by. He says he noticed the strained look on my face and asks, "What's up?" I tell him what I am struggling with. He inquires about the case I am writing about. I give him a copy of it, and after skimming it for a few minutes, he asks me a few questions that open my eyes to the conclusion I previously failed to articulate no matter how hard I tried. His brilliance astonished me.

For the bar exam, Mick told me that Eli did not go to any of the review classes and played basketball whenever he could during the weeks leading up to the two-day exam. He passed the bar exam on his first try.

I passed too, but I went to the review classes, took copious notes and spent hours each day up to and including the day before the exam studying and doing sample essays and multiple-choice questions.

Eli would join a small law firm that handled mostly assigned-counsel work, defending insurance companies in personal injury and accident cases. He bounced around such firms his first ten years of practice, did exceptionally well in cases that got him excited, but was lackluster handling routine cases and cases where he thought the injured party should prevail.

He then changed sides to join a firm that brought personal injury cases on behalf of injured parties. With those cases, he excelled, again, when something tweaked his interest, and barely did much for cases with dubious claims. He got himself fired and then joined other firms, until he finally just opened his own practice, once his kids were off to college. He refitted one of their bedrooms as his office, with a desk, a computer, and a combined printer/scanner/fax machine.

If his family had to rely on Eli's meager earnings alone, it would have barely scraped by. Fortunately for Eli, his wife Lucy is ambitious and, as the kids got older, she got her MBA from NYU and worked her way up the ladder at "one of 'em Morgans," as Mick would say, not sure if she was at the securities desk at Morgan Stanley or JPMorgan Chase. With Lucy's income, their kids were able to go to such schools as Tufts and Cornell.

When Eli's folks died, and they both died within a year of each other, he greatly scaled back his law practice, for he—an only child—inherited a small fortune from his parents that gave him almost complete financial independence, freeing him up from having to work full-time. This could have freed up his wife similarly, but Lucy liked her career, lacked significant interests in any hobbies or the arts, and was reluctant to be at home doing little else but clash with Eli on a daily basis.

And then soon thereafter, Eli won a case that resulted in such a windfall recovery that, but for his wife's insistence that he continue to maintain at least a semblance of a law practice, Eli really did not need to work any longer. Colleagues familiar with that case told me that Eli knew more than the defendant's expert witness, a supposedly renowned doctor held in high esteem by the medical and legal communities. I was told that Eli took the so-called expert to school. Eli was motivated in great part by outrage over how the other side mistreated his client, and in part by the low regard they mistakenly showed of his own legal abilities. It was at this point that he moved his office, and his now meager law practice, to D'Amato Café.

This financial freedom also gave Eli the ability to pursue his true interests, sports as both a spectator and player (basketball, of course) and music, especially, old-school soul and R&B.

◆

JENNY SAYS, "HE'LL ORDER a coffee, sometimes with something to eat, but not always. He'd be there on his cell phone talking away. Comes in with his computer and spends time looking like he's reading and writing emails, checking out websites too. Sometimes he bangs out long texts. Then folks—gotta be his clients—come to meet with him for an hour or so at a time.

"I was extremely pissed by his presuming he could just carry on like this without even saying a single word about it to me or Junior—or even to Frank Senior. But I know that Senior and Eli's dad Eugene were close cousins and said to myself that I'd better keep quiet until I talk to my father-in-law first. It's his store, you know.

"So, I go to visit Frank and bitch to him about Eli. He tells me, 'Let Eli do what he wants. Just make sure he don't interfere with the other customers and the business.'

"I tell Frank that being that the table he chose to set up shop is over in the far corner next to the kitchen, you don't even know he's here most of the time. But he has papers scattered all over the table and sometimes he tells the other customers to quiet down. He might be on the phone or with clients and he says the noise keeps him from being able to listen to what's being said. Other times, even when he's not on the phone or with anyone, but just sitting there or on his computer, he says he can't concentrate with all the noise.

"To this, Frank tells me, 'Listen, my cousin Eugene, Eli's father, was very kind and generous to me during his life. I cannot begin to tell you all that man did for me. D'Amato's Cafe would not exist without the help he gave me. He would never accept anything, but I'm old-fashion, like you'd call it, and I must pay my debts. Eugene is dead, so anything I can do to help his only child is one way I can begin to repay what I owe my dear, late cousin.

"'So, let Eli do what he wants. If he gets out of line, talk to him, but talk to him nice and make sure he knows he's welcome in the store, but he just has to understand that it's a business and we do have to keep our customers happy and make them feel comfortable. *Tu cabish?*'

"I tell Frank, 'Sure, I understand, but this place is hard enough to run without the distraction from his presence.

"Frank then says to me, 'Jenny, *mi cara*, my sweetheart, please, what I say is how it has to be. I started this place and now that I am an old man, I handed it over to you and Frank Junior to run. You and Junior live a good life. The place covers its costs and what you take home pays all your bills. You two even travel some, not a lot, I regret, but that's the price we pay to do this kind of business. So, please understand that this debt I owe my late cousin is part of the cost to run this business. Make Eli feel welcome but keep him under control. He is a good man. He's very smart; yes, very intelligent, but he can be, how do you say?, absentminded, yes, that's it. He's absentminded and sometimes you need to gently remind him that he is in a coffee shop after all.'

"So, what can I say or do but thank Frank Senior for setting me straight and helping me better understand the reality Junior and me have to put up with.

"Anyway, lots of time he'll get here in the morning, make some calls, take some calls, look like he's answering emails, then leave and come back hours later."

I say, "When he is out like that, does he turn off his computer and secure it somewhere?"

"You know, I was telling Junior that I thought it strange that Eli'd just get up and go out, not say a word to any of us, not even Iris, the waitress he usually pesters, and just leave his papers scattered all over the table there and not even turn off his computer. Iris says it stays turned on to wherever he was when he leaves. This has given some customers, who are not regulars and aren't aware of what's going on with Eli, the impression that his computer is a public computer for them to use while they're here. Every so often Iris has to chase folks away from his computer, especially kids who log onto gaming sites."

This makes me wonder: "You wouldn't happen to remember Eli's coming in with a different computer than his own one day a little while ago, do you?"

"No. To keep my blood pressure down, I pay little attention to what Eli's up to, but Iris might. She called in sick and said she got a doctor's appointment now, but I'll have her call you when she's back. Should be tomorrow."

"Please do, thanks."

CHAPTER 10

"I'm afraid to think of the 'something else' possibility."

"**AL, RICHIE JUST CALLED.** You need to call into the conference call Mick asked me to set up."

"Conference call? I know nothing about a conference call."

"I emailed you with the appointment."

"As soon as I got back from D'Amato's, I had to deal with those Feds who were here waiting for me."

"Yeah, they arrived just before you returned. I got tied up with other stuff and figured you'd check your email. Anyway, Richie said all hands are on deck, waiting on you. So call in pronto."

Shit, I was not ready for this, but I dutifully call into that conference call.

I say, "Sorry, guys. I just became aware of this call. I was out all morning at D'Amato's and then there were two FBI agents here when I got back, and I was tied up with them until not long ago. I haven't even eaten my lunch."

Mick says, "Well, ain't that a shame. Listen, Richie, Julius and I got lots of other things to do. We need to know what you found out, so we can move onto next steps. Tell us what you learned at D'Amato's, then about your meet with 'em Feds."

Richie says, "Wait, why didn't you call and conference me into your talk with those agents? You should have told them I'm your attorney and any questioning could happen only in my presence."

"Sorry, Richie, but I didn't think of that, and honestly, under the circumstances, I have nothing to worry about. I haven't done anything wrong."

"Al, notwithstanding all that, they do not know that, and you need me to steer them in the proper direction, away from even thinking of the possibility that you or someone working on your behalf cleaned out those accounts in an attempt to rob that money and cheat the bank.

"Anyway, let's proceed in the order Mick just laid out."

"Okay. I went to D'Amato's hoping to catch Eli there. He didn't show, and Jenny said he's not there every day or for long on the days he does show up. His schedule is irregular.

"I did learn why he didn't show last night. He had forgotten until late that his basketball team had a make-up game. Lucy did email, but after I had already turned off my computer and after Francesca had gone home. We did not learn about it until this morning."

Julius says, "Yeah, talk of that game is all over the street. Eli almost started a riot, I hear."

Mick says, "That asshole's up to no good again. I ain't could friggin' understand why Lucy ain't stopped that lamebrain cousin of mine from playin' basketball. That asshole ain't realize when young street dudes get shown up on the court by a short, chubby, white guy in his fifties, who looks more like Mr. Magoo than Larry Bird, they gonna feel humiliated and disrespected and are gonna wanna save face one way or the other. Ain't could understand it, especially after Vernon and me saved his sorry ass that time at the court in the Village, where he scored the winnin' basket with a soccer header. Ain't for Vernon and me, the guy he covered wudda sliced and diced him real good. He wudda looked like a giant piece of Swiss cheese. You think he learns? Of course not, he's so hardheaded you'd think he's *Calabrese*."

Julius says, "And don't forget about that game in Philly. Eli's on that team that plays exhibitions against the Globetrotters. Not even a minute passes, Eli gets ejected for punching the Trotter center in the nuts, after one of his head-banger shots was ruled no good."

Richie says, "And then he goes into the locker room and calls Iverson out. The Philly police escort him to the Amtrak station with an order to get out of town quick."

Mick says, "Yeah, that fuckin' screwball calls me from Philly wantin' me to send one of my drivers to drive him from there back to Brooklyn. I tell him to go fuck hisself, but he cries to me that he ain't got enough money and Lucy ain't home."

I say, "How did he get there in the first place?"

"Who the fuck knows? He might of gone down to Philly with the team, then with all the mess he made and 'em pissed at him, they prob'ly told him to shove off.

"Anyways, like an asshole myself—you'd think I'd know better—I call and take poor Sammy away from his wife and kids on his only day off. He rushes down there, musta wasted four hours and more goin' back and forth, lots of the way through heavy Sunday traffic—no fun, I know. Then, Eli's got the fuckin' nerve instead of goin' into his house to get the dough to pay Sammy for the ride and his tip, gives poor Sammy a load of jive that I agreed to settle up face-to-face with Eli. Well, guess what happens? I pay Sammy four bills outa my own pocket and ain't even get *u' cazz* from Eli, that cheap son of a bitch. You think fuckin' Eli even calls and thanks me for bailin' his unwelcome ass outa Philly? I ain't even see the dope, not 'til I run into him on the street a week later, and the dummy's like he ain't even know me. That no-good friggin' piece of crap.

"I says to myself, I shudda gone to get him myself, be sure to get paid, but then I'd be so pissed at that no-good, motherfuckin' *disgraziat* that I'd end up killin' the chump, and with my luck end up as a cellmate with that dick Gilbert."

Richie says, "If it's any consolation, that wouldn't be possible. Gilbert's in a federal lock-up; murder would land you in a state penitentiary."

"Well, like they says, there's a silver linin' to even bad shit.

"Okay, let's quit wastin' time with that screwball's bullshit that ain't got nuttin' to do with this problem we—'cuse me—Al here got.

"What you find out today, Al?"

"In truth, not a hell of a lot. Jenny says she ignores Eli whenever he's there. The waitress Iris handles Eli's table and interacts most with him, but she's out sick today and at the doctor when I was there. I'll talk to her as soon as I can catch her; that should happen later today or tomorrow. And Francesca has continually been trying to reach Eli, even Lucy, without any luck."

Mick says, "Like I says to you earlier, cuz, you gotta shake and bake and get to the bottom of this. We're all guessin' that whatever happened happened when Eli had your computer. Ain't even sure that that's it. So, we gotta know what's up quick."

Julius says, "Yeah, that way I could figure out what I need to do to get to the bottom of what happened."

Richie says, "Okay, now, I want to hear what happened between you and those FBI agents."

"Well, they asked me all kinds of things, mostly in what looked like an attempt to see if there were any reasons why I'd have done the transfers and then pretended that someone else did. They wanted to know if I was in any kind of financial straits. They said they will arrange for what they called a forensic audit to assess my current financial situation."

Richie says, "They want to see if there were exigent circumstances which may have motivated you to steal this money. That's what was behind the bogus transfers of a couple of the other attorneys who were prosecuted. For some others, they were simply thieves who wanted easy money, to take something that wasn't theirs.

"Give me those agents' names. I'll run them by Adams and Zachs, our friends at the Bureau. We have to head this off at the pass, by laying out to them exactly what happened. Otherwise, they'll drive us all nuts, because they operate on a mode of being suspicious of you until we can give them reasons to remove the suspicion. Hence, it's critical to get to the bottom of this, to ascertain if this mess is related to something that happened to your computer while in Eli's possession or to something else."

Julius says, "I'm afraid to think of the 'something else' possibility."

Mick says, "Well, Al here will soon have an answer for us. Right, Al?"

"Yes, of course, Mick. I'll do my best to get hold of Eli and Iris and learn what I can."

Mick says, "Don't give me that 'do my best' bullshit. That's just a *sfaccim* excuse. You're gonna fuckin' get hold of that asshole Eli and drag outa him what the fuck happened durin' the time you made the mistake of lendin' him your computer.

"Eli's number one. But do check with that Iris to see if that ditz Eli had the computer sittin' there while he was in the bathroom or outa the shop. Somebody may of got to it while he was gone. That jerk Eli may not even know if somethin' like that happened. Iris may of seen somethin' that could answer some questions.

"I know that Iris. And I know her mom Valerie. Helped her out once. They're good people."

I say, "You know, Jenny did say that Eli does leave the place for a while every so often, and she says that Iris needs to snap at folks to keep away from Eli's computer."

Mick says, "See, didn't I friggin' tell you, you ain't could trust that screwball Eli. Real smart of you, cuz, thinkin' you can trust that schmuck withcha computer."

CHAPTER 11

[It] hits the fan on all conceivable fronts.

ON THE NEXT DAY, the shit hits the fan on all conceivable fronts: Iris, Eli, Mary Woodley, the New York Lawyers' Fund for Client Protection, the Grievance Committee governing attorney conduct in Kings County, the FBI, and (last but not least) Mick.

First thing on my agenda that morning is to get to both Iris and Eli. So, I call Francesca and tell her I'll be getting in later in the morning after I stop by Eli's and D'Amato's.

No one's home at Eli's. And I get voicemail all around when I call both Eli's and Lucy's cells. I then call Francesca and direct her to call, text and email both Eli and Lucy on a regular basis until she's able to touch base with one of them. It's just so frustrating and upsetting. I wonder how I'm ever going to get to the bottom of this.

I tell myself not to despair, as Iris may provide some useful information about what transpired the day Eli borrowed my computer. And, who knows? Eli may be at his "office," though doubtful, given he didn't answer his cell when I just called.

As I arrive at D'Amato's, the morning rush is dying down. I don't see Iris and the only thing at Eli's table is the Reserved sign.

Jenny sees me and says, "If you're looking for Eli, you forgot he doesn't get here 'til later in the morning. That's if he's coming."

I say, "Where's Iris?"

"Oh, Iris. Her mom called me last night. They think she might have mono, was gonna keep her in the hospital, but she got them to release her. Iris's staying at her mom's 'til she gets over whatever's the matter with her."

"Any idea when's she coming back to work?"

"Your guess's as good as mine, Al. You know anything about mono? That's assuming that's what she's got."

I mutter "Shit" to myself and ask, "Where's Iris mother live?"

"Someplace out on Staten Island."

"You have her number? I need to talk to Iris."

"The mother did not leave me her number but let me call Iris's cell and see if she picks up."

Jenny calls and when she lip-synchs "voice mail" to me, I jot down my cell number, so she could leave a message for Iris that I need to speak with her.

I thank Jenny for this help and head to the office. What little hope I felt from being able to get some information from Iris is now replaced by an enhanced sense of despair.

As I walk into the office, Francesca is on the phone and signals that the call is for me. Hoping that it's Iris calling me—I forgot she only had my cell number, I rush to my desk and pick up the phone.

It is Mary Woodley.

The child support proceeding I brought against Gordon Gilbert concluded with his paying Mary and her son, Roger, $750,000, plus another $75,000 to cover legal fees and other costs. All of those, including principally me, entitled to a portion of this latter fund refused to take any of it. We wanted Mary and Roger to have it, but she refused. Rather, it was agreed that those funds be placed into my escrow account and used to help people in need, with decisions on distribution to be made by a committee consisting of Richie, Mick, Malcolm, Pedro and me. Of the $750,000, Mary drew on $50,000 of it, and asked me to deposit the balance into a separate special escrow account I opened for her. Mary wanted to first consider her investment options before deciding where to invest those funds. She figured it would be safest if the funds were held by me in an interest-bearing escrow account pending her decision.

While knowing that all of my accounts, including all of my escrow accounts, had been raided and cleaned out, I had somehow suppressed—or perhaps repressed, whatever the difference may be between the two—the fact that Mary's $700,000, plus the $75,000 "help" fund, were now gone, and since learning of this mess days ago, I still had no clue how it happened and even less of a clue of how the mess was going to be fixed.

Not even the possibility of prosecution had caused this nightmare to transition from being a terrible dream to a dreadful reality. Not until now, that is.

"Hi, Mary."

"Hey, Al, hope you're well. And how's Mick? Tell him Roger's been talking up a storm about him."

"That's great, Mary. How can I help you?"

"You okay, Al? You sound preoccupied. Not like you."

"You know me well, Mary. I'm dealing with a serious problem, and I've been having a real struggle just trying to figure out how it happened and how to fix it."

"I'm sure Mick will lend a hand and help you out. You needn't be so stressed. Tap your cousin's resourcefulness."

"Oh, Mick's involved. So is Richie Abbatello and Julius, Mick's IT guy. You never met him, but you may recall Mick talk about him."

"Sure, he's the one who created that secure email network among us. So, you're in great hands with him and Mick and Richie."

"This thing has us all baffled, and it has quite serious ramifications which the mystery of what's behind it only makes worse."

"Sorry to hear that. I can see it has you troubled. I know you need to respect client confidences, so I won't pry. I'll tell you what I am calling about and then leave you alone, unless there is any way I can help."

"Okay, why don't you tell me what I can do for you."

"I decided on how I would like to invest those monies of Roger's and mine."

"Stop right there. I have to inform you, Mary, that that's part of the problem that I'm dealing with."

"What are you talking about, Al?"

"To cut to the quick, ..."

"Yes, please do. I'm beginning to get a bad vibe."

"All of my accounts, personal, business and escrow, including the special escrow account in which your monies were deposited, were emptied out by someone who apparently stole my identity."

"Holy shit! What does that mean, Al?"

"Well, I can't really tell yet. Right now we haven't a clue as to how it happened. There are some leads we're tracking, but we've not yet been able to put a finger on anything."

"You report this to the police?"

"I haven't, but the bank's investigation unit reported it to the FBI, as my bank, Charter Bank, is federally chartered."

"Isn't the bank responsible when there is a hack? How is identity theft different?"

"To lay it out to you, Charter Bank's investigator is taking the position that I may have done this and transferred the money into some untraceable offshore account, in order to steal it all; essentially, the suspicion is that I took what's there in order to get Charter Bank to replenish it. He says that even if that proves not to be the case, the bank may take the position that the identity theft arose due to negligence on my part, which would free Charter Bank from any responsibility. The investigation is still pending, so we do not know what the bottom-line will be as far as Charter Bank is concerned."

"That's screwed up, but how about FDIC protection?"

"FDIC insurance would only cover $250,000 per account, but in truth I don't know if that coverage kicks in when it results from identity theft and not bank failure."

"That sucks. Doesn't the state have protection for escrow accounts?"

"Yes, but that usually kicks in when an attorney steals the money, which I absolutely assure you is not the case here. If it did cover this situation, you'd have to make a claim, but the maximum recovery is limited to $400,000.

"Now should you need some of the money in the short-term, between Mick and me, you will be covered."

"But, from what I am gathering, in the long-term Roger and I could be back to square one without enough money for me to complete my education so I can adequately support us.

"Shit, Al, I don't know what to say, except I relied on you once when I was desperate, and you came through. Is this screwup or whatever with your money an indication that my relying on you, my faith in you, was misplaced? I sure hope not and pray that you rectify this. It would be horrendous if after all's said and done, I end up no better off than before.

"And when were you going to tell me this? If I didn't call, would you have kept it hush-hush?

"This is all too upsetting and unsettling. I have to get off and calm myself some. Let me know once you know what the fuck's going on and if there's anything I need to do."

"I am so terribly sorry, Mary. Please, we are working to get to the bottom of this and to fix it, and I hope and pray that at the end of the day all will be straightened out, and you especially will not lose even a cent."

"I sure hope that's the case. The last thing I want to do is to sue you or get you disbarred. Roger's and my well-being is my first concern. You understand that, don't you?"

"Of course, I fully understand and respect that. And I assure you that we didn't fight as hard as we did just to let that money slip through our fingers—uh, my fingers."

"But, wait. You don't think Gilbert's behind this, do you? To get his money back and for revenge against us?"

"You know, until you just mentioned it, that possibility never crossed my mind. The last couple of times I saw him, when he was arrested and when we settled the child support case, he was a dejected and defeated man. So, that gives me major doubts that he possibly could have a hand in this. He's in prison, and it would be extremely difficult to swing something like this even if he were more defiant in defeat."

"I sure hope you're right, Al. But he knows that the $750,000 was wired directly into an escrow account you set up for Roger and me."

"At the time the funds were to be wired into my account, I mentioned to his attorney that the money would be there temporarily, until you decided how you wanted to invest it. So, as far as Gilbert would know, those funds would no longer be there."

"Okay. Perhaps that does eliminate Gilbert as a suspect. But I have to tell you, as perverse as it may sound, his being behind this would provide some comfort, because—based on what I'm hearing—it would remove the disturbing mystery behind the disappearance of my money, and which makes this so terribly troubling.

"Listen, I have to go. This is so fucked up and is giving me a migraine. Goodbye."

"Bye."

Great!

As soon as Francesca sees my call is over, she comes over and drops off a FedEx envelope. I see it's from the New York Lawyers' Fund for Client Protection. The envelope contains a letter informing me that the Fund was notified by Charter Bank about what had happened with my escrow accounts. The Fund's letter orders me to inform the Fund in writing within seven business days what caused those accounts to be emptied. I am also ordered to provide an account to the Fund regarding the clients and others whose monies were in the emptied escrow accounts and the respective amounts involved. The Fund's letter also reminds me of my obligation as a fiduciary to inform those who had escrowed funds with me, whether my client or not, of what transpired and to also inform them of their rights with respect to the Fund. The letter cites to a particular section of the state's code of ethics which states that if I do not comply with this order within seven business days, the Fund will refer my failure to the applicable Grievance Committee for any discipline the Committee deems appropriate.

Great!

As I finish reading the letter from the Fund, Francesca buzzes and tells me there is someone in the waiting area who needs to hand me something.

That person is someone sent by the State of New York Grievance Committee covering attorneys in Brooklyn (Kings County). That Committee was also notified by Charter Bank, as well as by the Lawyers' Fund for Client Protection, of what had transpired with my escrow accounts. The Committee's letter to me orders me to respond in writing within seven business days to a series of questions, all intended to get to the bottom of this mess and of the steps I am taking to rectify it. The order notes that my failure to respond in a timely fashion would be deemed professional misconduct and subject me to appropriate discipline, including the immediate suspension of my law license.

Great!

The next thing I know, one of the FBI agents who visited me the other day is standing before me. Obviously, the FBI can walk right in without introduction.

The agent hands me an order that "based on probable cause" I am to surrender my passport within twenty-four hours. The agent said that unless I have the passport on me, he will be back the same time tomorrow for my passport. He points out the portion of the order which states that if the passport's not handed over within twenty-four hours, I would be subject to immediate arrest.

Great!

Shortly thereafter, who should stop by to visit, but my cousin Mick.

I fill him in on what happened so far today with Eli, Iris, Mary, the Client Protection Fund, the Grievance Committee, and FBI.

Mick says, "I'm tellin' ya, ain't this life grand.

"For the second time in our not so long lives, I, Michelangelo Rodrico Forte, get to say to my cuz, Alphonsus Salvatore Forte, that he's gettin' fucked without enjoyin' the pleasures of gettin' laid.

"Now, you asshole, you listen and you listen good. You gotta straighten this shit out before you find your ass behind bars once again. Actually, both behind bars and withcha little law license gone bye-bye. I'm tellin' you, I ain't could pony up all that dough you supposed to be holdin' for Mary. You think I'm Fort Knox or can just print money?

"This ain't no one of 'em I'm-so-sorry-but-I-tried-my-best-but-couldn't-fix-it deal. Your license's on the line, and if you can't get this dough back, poor Mary and little Roger are back to where they begun, desperate and with no place to go. And all that thanks to you and you alone. You just might do some time again in some joint. Only this time it's gonna be for real. And, who knows, this bein' a fed case, you might be bunkin' withcha buddy Gilbert in that federal pen.

"Get hold of that Iris, track down that stinker Eli, find the fuck out how this mess happened, or you'll be fucked forever and every which way. And I ain't even could imagine what Theresa's gonna do when she hears about this *budell.*"

Great!

CHAPTER 12

Finally, a lead.

"HELLO, THIS Mrs. Marchetti?"

"Hey, damn it, you ain't supposed to be botherin' me with no phone call. I'm on that don't-call list."

"No, I'm not soliciting you. I'm Al Forte from the neighborhood. I'm an attorney."

"You from the neighborhood, you say. So the fuck what? Know how many con artists, perverts and lowlifes come outa South Brooklyn? You say you're a lawyer. What are you some kinda shyster my soon-to-be-ex hired to try and get some of my money?"

"No. I am not Larry's attorney."

"Then, you gotta be shylockin' for some folks Larry owes money to, probably forged my name, and you wanna get me to pay."

"No, ma'am. I'm calling to speak to your daughter, Iris."

"Why you wanna bother that sick child for? And why you callin' her with this number? It ain't hers."

"I'm sorry to bother you, but didn't Jenny from D'Amato's call you to say I'd be calling to talk to Iris?

"And don't you remember me? We went to Sacred Hearts the same time."

"Oh, wait. Shit, yes, that's right, Jenny did call. I'm so worried about my sick Iris that my mind ain't right. Sorry.

I forget who she said was gonna be callin'. And, Jesus, you expectin' me to remember all the *strunzes* I went to grammar school with? Shit, lots of stuff happened since.

"Wait, ain't you Mick Forte's cousin?"

"Yes, Mick Forte and I are cousins."

"You know that Mick's a blessed saint."

"Yes, lots of folks from the neighborhood think highly of him."

"Wasn't for Mick, we ain't be havin' this here conversation."

"I called to have a word with ....'

"My soon-to-be-ex came over to bug the shit outa me one night when I was still there in Brooklyn. This was after I even gone to court and got this Order of Protection sayin' he can't come, I don't know, so close to me. What? Fifty feet? Whatever. Can't even wipe your ass with that worthless piece of paper.

"Anyways, Larry and me, we really get into it. Not just yellin'. He's hittin' me, I'm bitin', kickin' him. The whole block could hear the commotion.

"My neighbor, Veronica Giambini, knows about the Order. She calls Mick. She knows him real well, they real close; he's helped her kid, husband, everyone in that family. She knows he'd get there faster than the cops. She calls 'em after she calls Mick.

"So, Mick gets there real quick. Tries, but ain't able to talk no sense to Larry. You see, Larry ain't from the neighborhood, so don't really know Mick. Musta thought he could take him. Mick's short, you know, and a little chubby, but please don't tell him I said that about him. Larry don't think Mick's tough, and that asshole fool makes the mistake of goin' after Mick, who beats the livin' shit outa him. Don't know why we say 'livin' shit'? Shit's alive? Anyways, listen to this: Mick actually kicks the shit outa Larry; that dirtbag drops a load right then and there. The place stunk so much; was terrible.

"So, the cops finally get there and take Larry away. And I get stuck cleanin' up the stinkin' mess.

"Now, my aunt knows how bad I'm doin' and how I need to get away from my ex. So, bless her, she tells me to come and move to this place, here in Staten Island, and get started on my own. And it was Mick who moved my stuff here. He got me the truck and his guys did the move.

"Said to me his guys were all ex-cons but could be trusted. He guaranteed it. Normally, I wudda said 'thanks but no thanks,' but it was Mick. So I knew he'd back up what he says. And the movers he sends, one's white, one's Spanish and one's one of 'em Negroes. Now, most of us in the neighborhood growin' up and even 'til now, stay with our own, ain't have much to do with other kinds a people, if we can help it.

"You know, I learned a lot from the day of that move. These guys, rough and tough as they looked, with their tattoos, muscles, hairdos, 'cept for the guy with the shaved head—scary too, if you ran into any of 'em on an empty street when it's dark—'em guys couldn't of been better behaved gentlemen. Mick told me that he'd take care of everythin', that I owed him and his guys nuttin'. I ain't got much money, but I ain't no charity case. So, besides orderin' some pizza and beer, so they don't go home hungry and thirsty after workin' so hard on such a hot, humid day, I hadda give these guys somethin' to show my appreciation. I was ready to give 'em twenty bucks apiece, but they each smile at me real cute and say they appreciate it very much, but the pizza and beer was already above and beyond and not necessary, and the honor of helpin' me was more than enough for 'em. They ain't took the money. I cried like I never cried in my life, this was so sweet of 'em. That day changed me; got my eyes opened some.

"Anyways, it ain't been easy here on my own. I work two jobs, for this store durin' the week and waitress for a diner not far from here on Friday and Saturday nights, but my aunt she don't charge me much rent, and I don't waste the few bucks I make. And Iris is on her own. Goes to school at night and works over at D'Amato's. Lives with a roommate at a family friend's place for almost nuttin'. So, she does all right, 'cept now she's so sick."

"Jenny tells me they think she has mono. I hope she's getting better."

"You ask me, those doctors ain't really got no friggin' clue what the fuck she's got, but I forced her to come and stay here, so I can keep an eye on her and make sure she gets back on her feet."

"Do you think I can have a quick word with her."

"Wait. You says you're a lawyer and you're Mick's cousin. You ain't that pain in the ass *chooch* that bugs the hell outa Iris at work?"

"No, Mick has two cousins who are lawyers, me and Eli Ativa. You and I went to school together. Eli's from the neighborhood too but went to public school. It's Eli who runs his law practice from D'Amato's."

"If both you and this asshole Eli are Mick's cousins, how come your last names ain't the same?"

"That's because Mick's dad and my dad are brothers, and Eli's mom and Mick's mom are sisters. Eli and I are not related."

"That goddamn neighborhood is somethin'. Everyone's connected with each other in so many different ways.

"Anyways, it's real nice to talk with you, Al, but again why you callin' me?"

Luckily, we are on the phone, and Mrs. Marchetti can't see me roll my eyes and shake my head in astonishment.

I say, "I need to ask Iris a few questions."

"About what?"

"About something that she may have witnessed at work."

"Listen, she's real sick, and really's not up to gettin' involved in no legal mess."

"No, I assure you, Mrs. Marchetti...."

"Al, it's Valerie, doncha remember?"

"Of course, I remember. Your full name was Valerie Valentino. Not easy to forget a name like that."

"Yeah, you remind me I gotta get rid of this Marchetti and get back to my family name."

"So, Valerie, can I speak with Iris?"

"Oh. I don't know. Let me see if she's up to it. Give me a sec."

After maybe five minutes, Valerie gets back on the phone.

"Al, listen, she's real weak, but says she heard from Jenny the information you need from her. Says that was her last day before she got sick but remembers that that Eli had a different computer with him that day. She says he got up and left all kinds a papers thrown all over the table he uses for his office and left with that computer still on."

"She say anything about anyone using the computer."

"Hold your horses, I'm just gettin' to that."

"Sorry."

"Okay, now listen. She says 'cause it bein' lunch time she was busy and away from that Eli's table, but did catch this guy screwin' around with that computer."

"She say what exactly that guy was doing, and did she know who he is?"

"She says she ain't know what he was up to, but she went over to him and told him to stop messin' with that computer. Said it looked like he pulled somethin' outa one of—what she say?—some kinda slot."

"USB slot?"

"Yeah, USB, ABC, somethin' like that. And she says the jerk walked away with the little thing he took out."

"Okay, who was doing this?"

"She said she ain't really know the guy good. Says maybe Jenny or Junior there do. Says he's one of 'em wise guys, least she tells me that's how he dresses and acts like. Only goes to D'Amato's every so often; ain't no regular. Thinks they call him Red or somethin' like that. That's all she says she could remember."

"Okay, this is very helpful, Valerie. Please thank Iris for me and tell her I hope she's well soon. And thank you very much for your assistance here, Valerie. Sorry to take up so much of your time."

"No sweat, Al. Happy to help and give my love to that cousin of yours, Saint Mick."

"I sure will. Bye."

"Bye."

Finally, a lead. This gives me a ray of hope that I just may yet get to the bottom of this mess.

CHAPTER 13

"Stop with the excuses already."

"**AL, ISN'T THIS RED** the dude who got Mick jailed?" Julius says when I call him to inquire if he knew anything about this Red whom Iris said had removed something from my computer that day Eli borrowed it while in his "office" at D'Amato's.

I say, "I thought that guy's name is Alfred Russo."

"Street names. Italian hoods like street names. I think Red is Russo's street name."

"You mean nickname. I wasn't aware whether Russo had one. I called Mick, but the call went right to his voice mail."

"Yeah, he's overseeing some repairs. But JBJ knows Alfred Russo or Red too."

"Why's that?"

"He's just telling Mick this morning how Red's been harassing his aunt for the dough her dead husband owes him. This Red's scared her into giving him a thousand bucks from her husband's life insurance."

"Wait, unless she signed some marker or something to guarantee any debt her husband owed to this Red, she has no obligation to pay Red anything. And nor is Red entitled to any of her husband's life insurance for which she's the beneficiary. Besides, from what Mick's told me about her husband, JBJ's uncle, anything he owed were for gambling debts and those obligations can't be legally enforced."

"Well, according to Mick, this Red's cruisin' for a bruisin', and it's something that's now on Mick's radar."

I say, "Well, but how about what Iris said about this Red's removing something from my machine's USB slot. No doubt it was something he had inserted into my computer. Is there a device that would enable someone to access my files that would permit my identity to be stolen and all of my accounts cleaned out?"

"Depends, Al, on what's on your computer. Would you have stored account information there, even passwords? And how about your phone? Is your cell phone synched with your computer."

"Shit, yes. My cell is synched with my computer, and I keep a lot of account and password information there, figuring that's a convenient and secure spot for that stuff. But from what Scotto told Richie, the bank's claiming that whoever did the transfers used my computer to do it."

"New programs have been developed by some in the hacker community that could copy a computer's unique identifying data. The same folks also developed these slick, powerful devices onto which you can copy those programs, and that makes it possible for a computer's identity to be swiped. So, if that kind of device with those programs was inserted into your computer, it could access and copy your computer's identifying data, besides copying your files. If that were the case, someone could pull off what happened to you.

"And once someone has the identifying data they could create a clone of your computer. And doing it this way makes it look like you did it even though someone else is doing it using a different computer. And as far as anyone on the outside could tell, like the bank's investigators or law enforcement folks if they took a look, it was you closing those bank accounts using your passwords working from your own computer.

"In fact, I have no doubt that while those transfers were happening, texts were generated by the bank's security protocol sending verification codes to your cell phone directing that the codes be inserted where indicated to confirm it's you making those transfers; whoever was requesting the transfers would have had to insert those codes in order for the transfers to proceed. With your cell phone being synched with your computer, whoever did this could access those texts with the verification codes by the clone of your computer, insert those codes in the requests to make the transfers, and then erase the texts from your phone (by erasing the texts from the clone of your computer) before you noticed them on your phone. This all could've been done at night, while you slept. With the phone-to-computer synch, it could happen even when your phone's turned off."

"Fuck! What can we do to confirm that this is the case?"

"I'm going to have to think on that some, but it's not gonna be easy and may not even be possible.

"And, you know, I never met this Red, but from what I hear from JBJ, Red's one of your typical old-school wise guy thugs. I'd be surprised if he even knows how to turn a computer on. My guess is he must've been coached to do what he did, and I doubt very much that he has any clue of how to squeeze out the info needed to do what was done to you."

I say, "Okay, we'll have to call a meeting for you, me, Mick and Richie to talk this out. I'll have Franny coordinate a sit-down or conference call. In the meanwhile, knowing what we now know, you think we still need to get hold of Eli to see if he has anything to add to this?"

Julius says, "From what you say, Eli wasn't even in D'Amato's when Red did what Iris said she saw him do. Eli probably doesn't have anything to add about this, but we won't know this without first talking to him. He just still might know something that'll help us."

"Okay. I'll continue to try and get a hold of him. Can't for the life of me understand why he's been so elusive."

◆

JBJ GIAMBINI WAS HEADING down the road of being a lost soul, until a "lucky coincidence" got Mick and me to recruit him to be one of our spies behind enemy lines in the Gilbert child support matter. He was in the ideal position to assist us, because of his patronage position as Special Assistant to the then First Deputy Mayor, Gordon Gilbert. JBJ's legal name is Johnny Boy Giambini, Junior, but everyone in the neighborhood calls him JBJ. Family members call him Junior. Now that he is an adult, he's John to outsiders.

As a result of his helpfulness with Gilbert, JBJ developed some confidence and direction.

These days, whenever I run into his mother, she lunges at me with hugs and kisses, and she tells me over and over and over again how grateful she is for how I saved her son.

Forget about when she sees Mick. Mick's a saint and a hero as far as she's concerned; he's her family's savior. In fact, many in the neighborhood feel the same way, Mick's been so helpful to many in their time of need. Mick can't walk down either of the main commercial strips of Court or Smith Streets without a merchant running out with a bagful of groceries or booze or pastry or whatever, as tokens of appreciation.

It's at the point where Mick has to shop outside the neighborhood, as his money is no good on Court and Smith Streets and Atlantic Avenue too.

If he ever ran for political office, Mick would be a shoo-in. He never would want to do anything as "legit" as that, knowing how corrupt politicians are wont to be (or become) and as distrustful he is of the law because of who it really protects and because of his disdain for attorneys, except for yours truly and Richie Abbatello.

Soon after the Gilbert matter was resolved, Mick says, "You know, that JBJ, he done right by us. Turned out to be one of 'em diamonds in the rough; I think that's how someone like you'd say it."

"Yes, you're right, Mick. That would be an appropriate way to describe JBJ."

"Good. Thanks for the English lesson."

"Mick, come on, don't start."

"Okay. Anyways, 'cause of his doin' right by us, I decided I needed to do right by him.

"You know better than me that my property management business been growin' faster than I could handle it. I ain't know all 'em ins and outs about that business and was runnin' into trouble. Withcha help, I hire 'em consultants you told me are experienced managers with good reps, and they trained my crew real good. But they ain't could be available to us 24/7; they got their own stuff to do. So, when we had problems, we ain't could always get hold of 'em quick.

"So, when that prick Gilbert goes down, who knows what the hell's gonna happen to JBJ's job as Special Assistant to the First Deputy Mayor, or whatever the cockamamie title that kid had? So, I ask JBJ if he ain't wanna come and work for me and become one of my property managers.

"You see, I ain't was really sure why everybody, me too, think that he's one of 'em spoiled Italian momma's boy punks, like that Johnny Pinto whose ass you kicked back in the day."

"No, Mick, once again, it was Jackie Pintero and I really did not get to kick his ass."

"*Va fa cul*, whoever the fuck it was and whatever the fuck happened.

"Anyways, seein' how good JBJ followed our orders, how like a man he did what we needed him to do, I start to think that he ain't might not really be a lousy punk. Maybe he's one of 'em guys who needs to feel that folks believe in him, have confidence in him. I thought he might could do better if he gets a chance, and so I decide to offer him a job.

"So, you shudda seen the smile on his face when I ask him to come work for me and you should see how good he's turned out. He and my other managers and crew work real good together, and with the trainin' we got from 'em management consultants and stuff they learned on their own online and through contacts JBJ had with city workers from when he worked for that dick Gilbert, they now have my properties runnin' much more smoothly, especially with the paperwork. We were always good with repairs and shit like that, but that dopey paperwork bullshit that City Hall says we gotta do, it's a mystery to us before. Now, my people know what's gotta be done with all 'em forms and all 'em notices to the tenants and to city agencies and all the other rigmarole *med* they gotta follow, for whatever fuckin' reason I ain't never could figure out. And there ain't no more chaos to deal with, no fires to put out, and everythin' runs a whole lot better.

"You gotta know, big Al, what's there to learn in all this. Well, I know I gotta hadda said it over and over again, but listen to me some more. Maybe, just maybe, you learn somethin'. Even though I did some things to help JBJ and his dad and his aunt and uncle, 'em folks owe me nuttin'. I don't believe in that. I do expect that if someone needs help, even me, and you can help, even JBJ, you help. Lots of folks do this for their family or neighbors, or around here for other Italians. Me? You ain't gotta be a relative or a neighbor or even Italian. Like you know, I help blacks and Spanish folks, and these days even 'em folks from Africa and the Middle East too; I help 'em all and they help me too. You got helped by 'em too; don't forget about your stay in jail with Vernon, when he had your back and *nessun*, not a soul—not a guard, none of 'em degenerate inmates—bothered you none. And that thing with me, Malcolm and Pedro, what some call

The Alliance, we've helped lots of guys, ladies, and kids, of course, who need help. For some of 'em it was hard for 'em to get the help they need, especially 'cause some are convicts or addicts. We help 'em and keep our eyes on 'em best we could, to make sure they didn't fuck up and to make sure that others treat 'em right too. Now think about how much better this place we call earth'd be if everybody looks out for each other this same way.

"Hope it ain't no news to you that not alla us Italians are good people, not alla us could be trusted. Lot ain't could be. And a lotta other kinds a folks, even 'em called folks of color, are great people whom you can trust your life to. The truth is we all could learn somethin' from folks that are different from us, just gotta keep an open mind and you'd be surprised what you'll learn and how much better things'll be if different folks shared the things they have with those who're different from 'em."

◆

"RED? THAT FUCK Alfred 'Red' Russo is behind this fucked-up mess withcha accounts?

"Listen, ain't no doubt he's a no-good crook who ain't could be trusted. But, shit, he's so friggin' dumb, he ain't could know shit about computers."

I say, "Julius too said he'd be shocked if this Red knew his way around computers. But I didn't know Alfred Russo's also called 'Red.'"

"Alfred Russo, the fuckin' *disgraziat*'s called 'Red,' 'cause of the color of the hair he used to have when he was younger.

It's 'cause of that rat bastard that I got sent to jail for that year. That SOB Red owed me tons of money, told folks that I was a wimp 'cause I ain't could make him pay up; says I let him slide 'cause I'm too scared to shake him down. That fool ain't understand that I'm holdin' a mortgage on this apartment buildin' he owned. I even had this thing my foreclosure attorney says is an assignment of rents. Way it works, he ain't pay me, his tenants gotta pay the rent they owe him to me instead. I get it direct from 'em. And it's while I'm collectin' that rent that I come to find out that that low-life *sfaccim*'s chargin' his mother—his mama, you hear?— double the legal rent, so that his *puttana* whore of a girlfriend could live in her apartment right across the hall rent-free. That shit pissed me off lots more than his runnin' off his filthy, stinkin' mouth disrespectin' me.

"That asshole finally wakes up to what's goin' on when he tries to collect the rent and his tenants, includin' his mama, tell him they paid the rent to me already. They let him know about 'em notices they got from my foreclosure lawyer. Red got the same notices from my lawyer up the kazoo but musta ignored 'em all. That shithead's too lazy to read, that's if he could read.

"So, I run into this no-good, lousy piece of shit. He bitches about how I'm stealin' his rents, and I yell at him about how he treats his mother. He tells me that if I like his mother so much I should *va fa cul* his mother, and I fuckin' lose it. I grab this stick that's lyin' there and gave the *strunz* a good whack to his fat head. You ask me, that poor stick gets it worse than Red's thick skull. Of course, I ain't notice that Red's crooked cop cousin Vito's right there, sees it all and hauls me off to jail, where I spend what turns out to be the best year of my life. It's there that I meet Pedro and Malcolm, and The Alliance happens, and this helps to make me a better person—and even improves my businesses.

"Anyways, not too long ago Pedro tells me that Vito, that fuckin' crooked cop cousin of Red's, been harassin' the niece of one of Pedro's wife Manuela's friends; the girl bein' bothered's named Stella. Vito musta seen Stella walkin' down Columbia Street, goin' into her buildin'. He parks his squad car and follows her into the buildin' and to her apartment. He's in uniform, you gotta know. He asks Stella all kinds a questions. Finds out Stella's on welfare, is a single-mom of a little girl in kindergarten, and then molests her, sexually. Not rape (maybe that dick Vito ain't could get it up) but touches her where he ain't should and forces her to do things to him, she ain't wanna do. No clothes are on while all this shit's happenin'. Anyways Pedro's wife tells him the cop drops by every so often to molest Stella, who's scared shitless.

"This bein' a cop, Pedro and I ain't could just beat the livin' daylights outa him. So, I get together with City Council Member Carlo Ruisi and Precinct Captain Luongo and tell 'em what I know. I already talked to Julius, so I tell 'em that Julius'll set up one of 'em web cams in Stella's apartment to record what happens the next time this Officer Vito's there. Julius says he can set it up, so Stella could turn on the web cam as soon as Vito knocks on her door. Besides recordin' the action, turnin' the web cam on'll give Julius a signal on his cell phone. Captain Luongo gives me some special phone number for Julius to call as soon as Julius gets the signal, so Vito could be caught with his pants down by cops Luongo promises'll be there pronto to arrest this no-good scumbag.

"No sooner than the next day, guess who stops by to visit Stella? Vito knocks, Stella activates the web cam, Julius calls the magic number and then me, and the cops are escortin' Red's dirt bag cousin in cuffs just as I arrive.

"Carlo tells me that the cop union attorneys're sayin' they're gonna challenge the web cam; some bullshit about entrapment. I mention this to Richie, and he says that maybe it wudda been better if the DA had orchestrated the trap. 'Orchestrate'? I says to Richie, 'we ain't at no friggin' Carnegie Hall.'

"Anyways, it turns out that nuttin' was said about the web cam, 'cause asshole Vito ain't just confesses to all the shit he's done to poor Stella, but he fuckin' brags about it when they question him. Those union lawyers couldn't do shit to save dopey Vito or reduce his sentence 'cause that now former cop bein' such an ignoramus. Bein' stupid gotta run in that fucked-up family.

"Now, between Malcolm, Pedro and me, and the folks we know on both sides of the prison—the correction officers and the inmates—that Vito's gonna be his cellmate's choice *gooma* for a good long time.

"You know, I ain't could talk to you without also talkin' about everythin' else that ain't got nuttin' to do with the mess we tryin' to clean up. Let's get back to that. We gotta get hold of Red and drag outa him whatever we could."

I say, "That's not going to be easy. He'll probably lay low and avoid you altogether."

"Lucky for us, that *scustumat*'s a greedy, heartless bastard and there ain't no love lost between JBJ and good ole Red. Red, you see, would loan lots of dough to guys in the neighborhood with gamblin' problems. Then he'd squeeze the shit outa 'em to pay. That fuck knows how it was messin' up marriages and families, but he keeps squeezin' and squeezin' away, bleedin' 'em dry, to get his grubby hands on more and more dough. Red ain't got no fuckin' heart. Ain't no surprise; see how he treated his own mother.

"It's Red that did in JBJ's uncle. And JBJ's been tellin' me Red's botherin' his aunt."

"Yes, Julius said that he harassed her so much, she paid him a thousand dollars from her life insurance proceeds to get him off her back."

"You can be sure that Red'll be back for more."

"Not if he knows you have him in your sights."

"Well, Al, that dope ain't know of my connection with the Giambini family. JBJ's already contacted Red to set up a sit-down. JBJ told that fool his aunt'll pay Red the rest of the money owed him by her dead husband. Red ain't know that the agenda for that meet's gonna be changed.

"And, I'm lookin' forward for a chance to bada-bing that scumbag upside his fat thick friggin' skull one more time. And talkin' of bada-bingin', that goes too for that fuckin' asshole Eli. Any word from that jerk?"

"No, Mick, but with what we now know about Red, Eli may not have any information for us. It's likely he wasn't there when Red was screwing around with my computer."

"We ain't could know that for a fact 'til that schmuck Eli gets back to us. So, keep on tryin' to get that fuck and stop with the excuses already."

CHAPTER 14

"Where's ... Eli?"

"HI, AL, THIS IS Jimmy, Franny's husband."

"Oh, hi, Jimmy. How you and Franny doing?"

"We're very happy, Al."

"Wait, don't tell me. You're calling to tell me Franny had the baby, right? But, wait, it's weeks early, no?"

"That's right. We or the doctor must have screwed up the due date. The baby popped almost a month earlier-than-expected. Franny wanted me to call you right away, but she says that you don't have a thing to worry about. She's up to date with her work, and Caroline should be ready and raring to go to cover for Franny while she's out on maternity leave."

"Thanks, Jimmy. Give Franny my best. Once things get settled, I'll come over to see the baby. Wait, boy or girl?"

"Oh, yeah, I forgot to tell you. It's a boy and we're naming him Patrick."

"Patrick?" I wonder to myself: Why that name? My family typically names its children to honor a beloved relative. And there's no one named Patrick in the family; there were a Pasquale or two, but no one named Patrick.

"Oh, we're naming the kid Patrick after my best friend who died just around the time the baby was born this morning."

"Jimmy, I am so sorry to hear about your friend. And I didn't mean to question your choice of name."

"No sweat, Al. Franny and I know we'll have to explain our choice to the family.

"And my buddy Pat and I go way back, and he and Franny also developed a special relationship. Same goes for Abby, his widow, who's one very special lady.

"Honoring Pat in this way helps us to deal with the sadness we feel about Pat's sudden, unexpected passing. This news was starling, devastating, really. It's hard to balance the joy we feel with this sorrow.

"They think my friend Pat had pancreatic cancer."

"Oh, geez, by time they discover you have that cancer, it's usually stage 4 and there is not much hope."

"Yeah, I hear the same thing.

"You know, Pat was quite a guy. Genuine, no bullshit, solid in every way. Cared about folks. Did whatever he could to help. Was a community organizer when he was young, a damn good one and tough too. Learned his stuff in Chicago. Worked in Toledo and here in Bed-Stuy. That work took a lot out of him. You ask me, he burned out because of frustration over not being able to accomplish what he wanted for folks. Too many insurmountable barriers. Then he taught school for years. Took on the toughest kids and got through to many of them.

"Pat was basically a real simple, direct guy. Had no pretensions, made no excuses. Never allowed any of his limitations get in the way of the task at hand. Wasn't afraid of failing, just committed to getting the job done, move ahead, no matter what it took.

"He'll be greatly missed. He was one of a kind.

"Anyways, the timing of my pal Patrick's death and our Patrick's birth made Franny think of a line she liked from a song she heard when she was a kid, by a band you probably know, Blood, Sweat and Tears."

I say, "Of course I know them, even owned some of their albums. And I think I know the line you refer to. It's from a song they sung written by Laura Nyro, the singer, songwriter with terrific talent. She was from the Bronx; even went to the same school as Janis Ian, another one with fabulous talent whose songs spoke to us back then. Anyway, the line you refer to is from the song called 'And When I Die,' and goes something like: When I die and when I'm gone, there'll be one child born to carry on...."

"That's it, Al. You nailed it."

"No, Jim, you and Franny nailed it by honoring your friend Pat in this profound way.

"I'm proud of you both. What you've done is sure to bring some solace to Pat's widow.

"Okay, I know you have lots of other calls to make, Jim. My condolences for your pal Pat. And congratulations and blessings on Franny, you, and baby Patrick. I look forward to seeing you all soon."

And so my already complicated work life becomes further complicated by Franny's earlier than planned absence.

I arrive early to the office the following morning, and I am shocked to find the front door unlocked, the office fully lit, and a vibe of energy emanating from who knows where.

Sitting at Francesca's desk is Caroline Falconetti, who I know from my days at Gilbert & Associates, PLLP. Caroline also happens to be Francesca's aunt; she's Francesca's mother's sister. Caroline recently retired after being the executive assistant and legal secretary for some 37 years to Jake Porter, who together with Gordon Gilbert and Joan Zakorski founded G&A. Caroline followed Jake to each and every firm he moved to after the dissolution of G&A. She also followed him into retirement—at least temporarily.

I know Caroline to be a highly skilled, hands-on and take-charge legal secretary and had every reason to believe that she would pick up from where Francesca left off and run my office seamlessly during Francesca's maternity leave. Francesca had vetted Caroline fully and filled her in thoroughly, even before I had a chance to interview her, the mere formality of which became moot with baby Patrick's early arrival.

But Caroline and I do not exactly get off to a good start.

"Oh, welcome, Caroline. I wasn't expecting you to be here so early and wasn't even sure you'd be in today."

"Thanks for the welcome, but what the hell's going on here? During the last days of G&A, it was sheer chaos there. It was like working at a fly-by-night place. We had no clue if or when we'd get paid, and if paid, whether the check would bounce all the way to the bank or not. I mean, who could trust that greedy, demon Gordon Gilbert? He'd screw his own mother. There were plenty of intense moments then; just about drove me out of my mind. In the end we were paid. The word was the Executive Committee discovered that Gilbert had some slush fund and forced him to draw from that to pay us all. They threatened to rat him out to the bankruptcy trustee.

"It was like that too at a couple of the other places Jake and I worked after G&A's fall, but each of those sinking ships did manage to eventually cover my salary.

"I have to let you know that my helping you out while Francesca's at home puts me in a serious bind. Francesca said she didn't think she needed to tell me about the stolen monies issue, as you had assured her that that would be resolved if not by now then by time Francesca was expected to give birth, thought to be weeks from now. So, your financial mess is totally unexpected. If I had known about it, either I would have said no and stayed retired, or I would have moved my monies around differently.

"I had no idea I'd be facing here something like I faced at G&A and those other places. I have savings, but a lot of my money is tied up with my 401(k) and other retirement accounts, and I don't want to touch those accounts; I'm going to need them when I do finally retire. Since this job came up when it did, I held off collecting Social Security and decided to invest a lot of my fungible money into CDs, each of which can't be touched for a while without a penalty, and by that time Francesca will be long back.

"And my husband Mikie's auto repair shop isn't a money-maker. What he takes home is chump change and it's nothing like real pay no matter how hard he works. Whatever he does manage to bring home certainly can't support us.

"So, I'm the breadwinner in my family, and my helping you out while Francesca's not here puts me in a precarious position. I don't know what to do; don't even know if I can stay here if I don't get paid on a regular basis. I may have to find something else to tide me over. What the heck's going on here? Am I going to get paid?"

"I am so sorry, Caroline. What happened to my accounts was totally unexpected, but I am working furiously to fix it. Be assured that I take very seriously my obligation to pay you. I don't expect you to work for free, even if you were otherwise rolling in dough. And I need to keep our doors open, in order to generate income going forward.

"As I said, I am working on fixing things. I do have money squirreled away and my cousin Mick will float me money until this thing gets resolved. So, you have my commitment to make good on every penny that is owed to you. I made the same promise to Francesca, who's owed money while on maternity leave, as Jimmy's pay alone isn't enough to cover all their bills, especially now with the new baby."

While it is great to have a competent and efficient replacement for Francesca, the additional financial burden I assume by taking on Caroline during this financial fiasco—which I hope and pray is temporary and soon to be resolved, despite all signals to the contrary—is nerve-wracking. It only adds to my increasing anxiety, which is compounded by the prospect of an imminent nervous breakdown. While I'm not happy to take on this additional burden, as difficult as it would be for me to carry on my practice without this help, it would be impossible to do so now that I'm faced with the challenge of having to figure out and fix the mess I find myself in.

I feel screwed, I agonize. Where the fuck is that asshole Eli? (I'm such a mess that I'm starting to sound like Mick.) This problem resulting from the stupid, ill-advised, so-called solid I did for Eli can't get resolved without his getting me the information that I—and Richie, Julius and Mick—need to figure out who is at the bottom of it. Is it this mysterious Red? Someone else? We are in total darkness without Eli's shedding whatever light he can on who exactly is involved in this.

No one is home at Eli's house, neither he nor Lucy. And both continue to be strangely elusive, impossible to reach by phone, text and email. Calls, texts and emails to their two kids, who are away at out-of-town colleges, have not been responded to either.

I mutter to myself, "Where's that fucking asshole Eli?"

That night, I have a terrible nightmare. I see Eli and Lucy in the dark of night packing suitcases and placing them in their car and then driving off. My mind wonders: Is Eli behind this money-grab and has he run off with the funds stolen from my accounts?

When I wake up, I recognize that the thought that Eli robbed me is nothing but a bad dream. I know without a doubt that Eli had nothing whatsoever to do with what happened to my accounts. First, it's simply not in his character. He's incapable of doing anything like that. Secondly, were he ever tempted to steal from me, he knows that Mick would surely track him to the ends of the earth and slaughter him.

But then my conscious mind becomes consumed by a frightening thought: Is the disappearance of Eli and Lucy the result of an abduction by those who carried out the robbery of my accounts?

CHAPTER 15

"Taught Chubby Checker how to do the Twist."

"HI, MICK, GLAD YOU called. I finally heard from Eli. Except it was an email with a really cryptic message."

"Cryptic? What the fuck you talkin' about? He about to die or kill hisself? What the fuck does a crypt gotta do with anythin'?"

"No, no, Mick, a cryptic message is a message that is unclear."

"So, why ain't you just say that? What the fuck he say? Betcha he's gettin' cute with us. That friggin' no-good wise ass."

"Well, he wrote, 'Hear you're looking for me. I am not sure what you mean by what happened that day that I borrowed your computer. Nothing at all happened. Am tied up with something very important that's happening any day now, after which I'll have to lay low for a while. I'll be in touch once the dust settles.'

"That's all he wrote."

"What the fuck's that supposed to mean? And ain't you let that asshole know how important it is you talk to him? Can't that shithead just call you with a burner phone if he gotta stay all hush-hush, 'cause of some who-the-fuck-knows-what-kinda bullshit he's got up his sleeve? You gotta pin that friggin' airhead down or he keeps talkin' in circles."

This conversation transpires on a Saturday morning. While Eli's email resolves my ominous thought from earlier that morning, it does not eliminate the need for me to question him about whether he has anything to add to what I learned from Iris.

Mick calls me the following morning.

"Al, Sammy's sister, Shirley, was at this dance last night and thinks she seen that goofball Eli and even Lucy with some friends. Says 'em all dressed and actin' like they're the second comin' of the Blues Brothers.

"She's at one of 'em Rhythm Review dances that that guy on the radio, Felix Hernandez, throws every coupla months at different places. Last night's at a spot in the Village. Shirley says the place's packed and says this group of six stroll in like they own the damn joint, three guys and three gals, all dressed in dark suits with white shirts, black ties and shoes, wearin' black fedoras and with shades."

I say, "She sure that Eli and Lucy were part of this group?"

"Not a hundred percent, but she says it sure looked like 'em, especially Eli, from his size and the shape of his ugly body. Says it's so crowded and dark that she ain't could get close enough to get a good look or to talk to any of 'em fools.

"Says once a Twist song comes on, this group just took over the middle of the dance floor and put on quite a show. In fact, she tells me after a while everyone else just stopped dancin' and circled around and watched those airheads dance the Twist, especially the one that Shirley thinks is Eli."

"Doesn't Eli claim he taught Chubby Checker how to do the Twist?"

"Yeah, that's one of the pieces of jive he tries to run by folks. Says it's all in the ankles or some shit like that. You know for that bullshit about teachin' that dance to Chubby to be true, Eli'd wudda hadda be 11 or 12 years old when that wudda happened. How the fuck's that possible? A load of the usual crap from that *strunz*.

"Anyways, Shirley says the crowd went wild and was whoppin' and hollerin' for these jokers to do more.

"The leader, who she's pretty positive is Eli, screams for 'em to play *Mustang Sally*, and when it gets played, he pulls out some kinda cordless mic and it's like karaoke time, alla sudden. This guy just takes over the place.

"But, then, she says they play *Billie Jean* and this guy yells that they hadda stop the music."

"Why?"

"You ask why. You know why? And this is proof that that *pazz* of a cousin of mine was there. One of 'em other pieces of bullshit bunk that my jerk of a cousin tries to run by folks is that he developed the moonwalk. Says he called it the 'backslide' or some *u' cazz* like that. Claims some guy sees him make that move at a college dance and offers to pay him a thousand bills for it, but only if Eli agrees he ain't never gonna make that move again and ain't never gonna show or tell nobody how to do it. That schmuck Eli ain't ask the guy who's he works for. Only later finds out that guy's one of Michael Jackson's reps. Also, my dopey cousin ain't understood the kinda rights he done gave up, somethin' about 'em lastin' forever."

"Sounds like you're referring to perpetual rights."

"Yeah, that's it. Perpetual rights, and this's before Eli becomes a lawyer and says he ain't know at the time exactly what the fuck he's doin'. Not that that stinkin' turd knows what he's doin' after he becomes a lawyer. Anyways, now he bitches that for the chump change of a lousy thou, he walked away from millions. Cries he's ripped off, and if he knows he's dealin' with Jackson, wudda made sure he got his rightful piece of the action for hisself.

"Anyways, if he's drivin' and a Jackson song comes on the radio, right away that dope slams that radio off. I seen him do that.

"At this dance last night, as soon as *Billie Jean* gets played, 'em Blues Brothers imitators and wannabes just march outa the place and never come back."

"Mick, do you think that that dance was the 'something very important' that Eli mentioned in his email from yesterday morning?"

"No. I ain't could believe he'd need to lay low 'cause of some dumb dance. What's the big deal that he, Lucy and a handful of goofy friends go to a dance dressed up like the Blues Brothers? Ain't could be that."

"I guess you're right, and we still have to wait to find out what he's referring to."

"Yeah, time's fast runnin' out, cuz. JBJ set up that meet with Red for tomorrow night, and we'd be better off knowin' Eli's side of the story before then."

"In that email Eli does say he's not aware of anything happening to my computer while he had it. I know I need to question him, and I'll continue to do everything I can to get hold of him. I'm leaving messages on email, phone, text, and even stopped by his house a couple of times each day. Jenny and Junior promise to call if Eli shows at D'Amato's, and Francesca said the daughter got back to her, and Regina says neither she nor her brother Sal been in touch with their parents for the past few weeks, but Regina told Francesca that she and her brother will reach out and will get back to us if either connects with their folks. Don't know, something weird is going on."

"Weird all right, like close to a coupla million bucks out the door and we're clueless how or why. Once again, for the millionth friggin' time, you'd better give it a serious go to get to the bottom of this shit, pronto."

◆

EVERYONE WHO KNOWS Eli is aware that, in addition to his love of playing basketball, another of his great loves is old-school soul and R&B music. And he also likes to occasionally put on some sort of musical act, like this Blues Brothers-like performance.

And everyone who knows Eli is also well aware that he is very opinionated about his likes in music. Ask him what he likes, this is what he says, "Notwithstanding Don McLean and his *American Pie,* and no matter what a fine song that is, the day the music died is April 1, 1984. That's the day Marvin Gaye was killed by his father. You ask me, not much good music has happened since.

"There's been no music as good as the great stuff by the artists I love. I'm referring to Sam Cooke, Otis Redding,

Aretha Franklin, Gladys Knight. Also, there's Patti LaBelle (who taught me just about all the French I know) and Etta James. And let's not forget Al Green and Curtis Mayfield. And I also love the music of groups like the Four Tops and The Spinners, especially when The Spinners were led by Philippé Wynne. It's a scandal that The Spinners aren't inducted into the Rock & Roll Hall of Fame. You ask me, dirty politics is the only plausible explanation for that omission."

Mick would complain, "Ain't could understand why that asshole cousin of mine Eli thinks he's such hot stuff. He ain't nuttin' but hot shit, you ask me.

"Anyways, somebody once asks me what my cousin Eli looks like. I says, you really wanna know what he looks like? Here you go: That skeevy bastard's a short, pudgy four-eyes with a salt-and-pepper 'stache, but very little other hair left on his big fat head. He's been losin' hair like it's goin' outa style; his beam's been stuck in a recession for the longest time. And there's 'em droopin' eyelids, a miracle he could see. Eyebrows, maybe, just maybe, a lousy few black and white hairs stickin' out over each eye. Then those puffy dark bags unda his eyes; scary, you ask me. Ain't got enough fingers and toes to count all 'em wrinkles on his butt-ugly face. Even looks like he's got hisself a turkey neck. Then, his shoulders droop like an upside-down V, and his back slouches so much, he cudda played that hunchback in that there movie about that church over in Paris they named that college after; shame about that fire that almost burned it down. That asshole's got more new hair growin' outa his ears than any other place on his head. His forehead's so huge he could make a ton of dough rentin' it out as a movie screen; he'd be able to retire just on the popcorn income. Top of everythin' else, he's a low-talkin' mumbler. Nobody knows what the fuck's he's sayin' half the time.

"And he's always wearin' that ratty lookin' Brooklyn Dodger hat, worn jeans and sneakers in winter; T-shirt, shorts and sandals with no socks, in summer.

"That describes my asshole cousin Eli B. Ativa, attorney at law, in a nutshell.

"And with all this, that mutt with such an ugly puss thinks he's God's gift to whoever. Unbelievable, I'm tellin' you.

"Thinkin' of Eli makes it easy for me to understand why 'em lights get turned down low when the dirty deed gets done.

"And it's one helluva mystery or miracle how he ever got such a pretty, sharp lady like Lucy to marry him. Got no fuckin' clue how Eli pulled that one off. She not only married him, even had a coupla kids with him. Just thinkin' of what she hadda go through there gives me the heebie-jeebies, I gotta tell you."

I say, "Well, maybe he has some special power. You know, some kind of psychic power that attracts women to him. Like the 'Kavorka' that Kramer from *Seinfeld* supposedly possessed."

"Psychic? If anythin', it's somethin' psycho, you talkin' about that weirdo freak, Eli.

"However he got that poor Lucy to marry him, it ain't 'cause of no goddamn special power. That much I know. It's a mystery, ain't no doubt about that, but his havin' any kinda magical power ain't got nuttin' to do with it, that's the most God-honest truth if ever there was one. Psychic? That's a load of bullshit. He's psycho if he's anythin'."

CHAPTER 16

"Change of the meeting's agenda."

"THAT MEET WENT DOWN with Red last night, Al."

"Yeah, so how did it go? Red must not have been too happy to see you and for the change of the meeting's agenda."

"Yeah, it broke the fucker's heart. He was expectin' to be sittin' down only with JBJ and his aunt to pick up a nice piece of change, and he ain't was happy with my little surprise.

"You gotta know that this fuckin' Red thinks he's a tough guy, thinks he's smart. That jerk's nuttin' but a piece of shit, a punk, and a cry-baby. I tell JBJ all his aunt hadda do is yell at Red some, that dick wudda backed off and stopped botherin' her. He gets away with all kinds a stuff, 'cause folks make the dumb mistake that he's got muscle behind him and that he knows what he's doin'.

"People think his crooked cop cousin Vito's his muscle, 'cause that's how I got sent to jail. It's sad that's what folks think. That asshole Red was lucky Vito's there when I whacked him good 'cross his big, thick head. Pure luck. Otherwise, that fuck Red wudda gone home took a few aspirins and that wudda been that. Anyways, if folks know the truth, they know that Red ain't tough, ain't got no muscle behind him, and ain't nobody to be a-scared of.

"Anyways, he sees me and Dominic and Paolo, and just about shits his bloomers. Musta already told you, if you wanna give peace a chance in a situation where you might be gettin' it on, bring big, tough guys with you. That way nobody ain't wanna fight.

"Red thinks I'm only there about JBJ's aunt, and he knows if that's it, then his ass is grass and is gonna get mowed real good. I let him know that JBJ's aunt is only one of the reasons why I'm there. I tell him he gotta stay away from JBJ's aunt, that she ain't owe him shit. I then empty Red's pockets and hand over to JBJ the dough Red took from his aunt. JBJ leaves to return that money to his aunt.

"I then explain to that douche bag the main reason why I'm there. I tell him that if he tells me what I need to know, he'd walk out and have no problems with me.

"I says to him that word got to me that he did somethin' to my cuz's computer, and I gotta know what the fuck he done.

"You gotta understand that another reason why I brung Dominic to this meet is 'cause before he got religion, Dominic's a stone-cold hitman, one of 'em assassins. Everybody's afraid of Dominic. He walks down the street, folks usta run for cover scared he's gunnin' for 'em. He ain't could buy no sandwich even; he goes into a store, everyone works there's duckin' unda the counter to hide.

"Shit-for-brains Red, of course, knows about Dom's rep, but he ain't know that these days Dom ain't hurt a fly. Red's scared shitless of Dominic. So, Dom's bein' there's like givin' Red some truth serum. Red's afraid if he lies, he dies, and he ain't want that to happen. So, he just goes ahead and lays it all out for us.

"He says, 'What do I know about these fuckin' computers? Ain't got no use for 'em. Don't know shit about 'em, don't wanna know shit about 'em, ain't wanna waste my time thinkin' about 'em.

"'This here guy comes outa nowhere, stops me on the street and wants to give me money to shove some gizmo up your attorney cousin's computer's hole. Don't know who the fuck this guy is and how he knows me. Says he asks around and folks in the know around the hood say I know my way around and am a stand-up guy. You know, could get stuff done.'

"That musta got Red hot; he's a clueless bum. And I know that guy's just bullshittin' that moron Red. Buildin' up his ego, so he could get that shithead to do what he needs him to do.

"Red goes on, 'This guy asks if I know you. I tell him, who ain't know Mick around here? Then he wants to know if I know your attorney cousin. Tell the guy I see your attorney cousin at D'Amato's alot. Tell him I even see him there working away on his computer. This gets the guy real interested. I tell him your cousin—never could remember his name—he'd be banging away on his computer and then sometimes just gets up and goes out somewhere and leaves the computer just sitting there and still on.

"'So, this here fella—think his name's George, something like that, I never was no good with names—asks if I wanna make some easy dough. I say that's the best kinda dough there is. He tells me all I gotta do is shove this gizmo he gives me into one of 'em holes in your cousin's computer, then the gizmo'll somehow do the rest.

"'Why your cuz and why his computer? I ain't got no clue. I'm guessin' attorneys got some kinda special programs that gotta be worth something. To tell the truth, I ain't even know what a program is, 'less you talkin' about TV programs, don't even care what the fuck they might be. But I do care about easy money, and this guy—what I say him name is? Gregory? No, George, that's it, I think—wants to give me a thou to shove this thing up some hole in that computer. So, I says sure.'

"Red then says, 'So, one day, I walk into D'Amato's and your cuz's there working on his computer. I'm halfway through with my double espresso, when your cuz gets up and walks out. So, I spring into action, shove that thing where that fella told me to put it, and before you know, this light on the gizmo that tells me my work's done shines. I take the thing out and get it back to that guy. He checks it on this tiny computer of his that he carries around, says I done good, hands me ten nice, crisp hundreds and then it's goodbye-nice-doin'-business-with-you. So, ain't nuttin' for you guys to press me about. Nuttin' bad happened to your cuz or his computer. I made a few bucks and that's that. You ain't could hold that against me.'

"I ask Red if my cousin knows what he had done to that computer. He says, 'Unless that waitress Irene, I think's her name, ratted me out, he don't know shit about what I done, and I never said nuttin' to him about it. To tell you the truth, I ain't even never said a word to the guy.'

"I says to him, 'From what you say, sounds like everythin's on the up and up. But next time somethin' like this comes up, you gotta come to me first or we're gonna have a problem. Hear me?'

"To this, that asshole says, 'Hear you loud and clear, Nick, no Mick. Sorry.'

"Red said he and this George, or whatever his name is, kept in touch only by phone and I passed on that guy's number to Julius, and he found that the number hadda be for a burner phone that's already ditched. Red said he ain't know where this guy hangs or lives or anythin' else about the guy.

"When I tell Red we was finished and he could go, I also say that if what he told to us checks out—I look at Paolo and Dominic, as I say this—then he goes in peace, as between us the past is the past: He welched on his loan, lost his buildin' to me, I did my time for smashin' his head, his crooked, now ex-cop cousin's on honeymoon upstate for messin' with Stella, and our lives goes on.

"So, Al, I ain't pressed Red any more, 'cause I ain't want him to get back to this George or whoever and let him know that he spilled the beans to us. I told Red that we'd keep this info between us, and he should do the same, and I made sure that Dominic stared him down good as I said this to him, and that punk Red shook his head back in Dominic's direction. I also ain't gave him no reason for tellin' nobody. You see, looks like he's told one thing, but he ain't know that the folks who got him to pull that crap withcha computer were really gunnin' to clean out alla your dough. Red thinks he's stole special lawyer computer programs, supposed to get resold. He only got paid chump change to pull off what he done. I know that cheap greedy bastard'll bitch up and down Court Street, and all over Brooklyn too, if he knows lots of dough got took usin' the info he sucked from your computer. He'd cry about bein' robbed and cheated outa his fair share of the action. And we ain't want this George and whoever else is behind this shit to know that we know about 'em and're after 'em."

"And that fool ain't know I got two lawyer cousins. He only knows my lawyer cousin from D'Amato's. Either this George ain't mention my attorney cousin's name, or he did, and it went in one of Red's ears and outa the other, as it usually goes with that *stunat* fool. But, as we know, by your lousy luck, whoever's behind this got my other lawyer cousin's dough. We ain't know if they targeted Eli to get to his inheritance or the bucks he got from that big case he won, or if you're the one they're after all along. That's one of the things we gotta find out.

"We'll need to get to the bottom of this, for there's gotta be more to it than we know. Get Caroline over there contact Richie and Julius to set up a meetin' to talk about where we go from here."

"We're on the same page, Mick."

CHAPTER 17

"Ain't want no publicity."

"No matter what, we ain't want no publicity about Red, so we ain't gonna say nuttin' to no cops about what he done and told us," Mick starts off the face-to-face meeting at my office with Richie, Julius and me that Caroline set up.

Richie says, "You sure about that, Mick? Folks hear about what Red did for that George—or whatever his name is—and that shows Al's in the clear. Red's arrest will take a load of pressure off. The bank's false suspicions will become baseless, the FBI will back off, and it'll be clear that Al's the victim here, so there'll be no reason for him to be disciplined by the Grievance Committee. Any suspicions of those who escrowed money with Al will be belied, and they'll have to stop bitching about him, and Al's clients' faith in his honesty and integrity will be restored. His practice will get back on its feet. And in the meanwhile, the cops or FBI arrest Red, grill him to establish what he's done and knows. Even if, as Mick believes, Red had nothing to do with the clearing out of Al's accounts, he did have the intent to aid in the theft of valuable computer programs for the unauthorized sale to others. That's a legitimate basis to charge him with a crime and arrest him. Even if it doesn't go anywhere, again, that helps put Al in the clear, and sooner rather than later."

"I ain't could agree with that less," says Mick. "Wrong thing to do, youse ask me. We need time to get to the scumbags behind takin' the dough from Al. Red's bullshit. He's just a dumb asshole workin' for easy money. Red's arrested and it's all over the news and papers, and this George, or whatever the fuck's his name, he's gonna know the cops and feds and us are gunnin' for him, and he's gonna lay low, or even skip town. Then, where the hell are we? Al's still out the money.

"Youse ask me, this thing ain't could be fixed as long as that dough's gone. So the fuck what, Al's a victim. Youse got folks outa money. It may not hurt alla 'em, but I know if any of my dough got took, I'd be plenty pissed and there ain't no excuses that's gonna make me not pissed. Then, doncha's forget about Mary and Roger. They'd be fucked without that money of theirs. This thing ain't fixed 'til that money's put back where it's supposed to be. And youse think the bank's gonna pony it up? Not without no fight, and what're the chances there, Richie?"

"Hard to say, Mick. You know, Al, what Mick says makes sense. If Red's arrested, it will very likely scare off this George and make it harder to get to those responsible for the real crime. If those responsible get caught, that provides the greatest possibility of recouping the lost monies.

"And I'm not so sure what we will accomplish fighting the bank. Even if we prevail, one thing I do know is that it's not going to be quick or easy. We're talking over a year. And I don't know if you'd win at all, and even if you do, you may not get all the money back. There's solid case law about recouping your personal funds, less solid regarding your business monies, and a dearth of case law about the loss of escrowed monies in the context of identity theft or otherwise."

I say, "So, Richie, what am I supposed to do? Chase after some elusive, unknown criminals? I don't have the capacity to do that, even with help. Meanwhile, as each day goes by, I'm getting more and more fucked. As you know, the bank's not budging an inch. As you mentioned the other day, the FBI is likely in the process of getting search warrants and will be executing them in the next day or so; those who had money in my escrow account are driving poor Caroline nuts each day, even their lawyers are calling threatening to file their own complaints with the Grievance Committee, even talking of going to the District Attorney. It's ongoing, and I'm hearing noise about established clients of mine looking for other attorneys to do deals that are now in the hopper, which I otherwise would be doing and getting paid for. It's distressing and I'm getting more and more stressed out."

Richie says, "I know it seems dismal, but I have to add that to bring a suit against the bank, while you and I can handle certain aspects of that, you will really need to bring in a high-powered firm with extensive experience suing major financial institutions who are deep-pocketed. In fact, if that's the route you decide to take, you must select one as soon as possible, because they'll need to evaluate your case every which way in order to advise you of how best to proceed. They may conclude that litigation would be too risky as to the result, or too time-consuming, or too costly. They may have alternative approaches, like negotiating a settlement with the bank or retaining private investigators to do a rigorous investigation as to the crooks behind the theft of your accounts and then turn over those findings to the bank and FBI."

Mick says, "Richie, stop this legal mumbo-jumbo and listen to me. We got good info from that jackass Red. We now know we ain't need to keep wastin' time chasin' after that *sfaccim* Eli. Based on what Red had to say, I ain't got no doubt in my mind that Eli's ain't know shit about what went down."

Richie says, "I have to agree on what you say about Eli. If he were aware of the theft—despite all the negative stuff you spout about him, Mick—I'm confident he'd be front and center and helping any way he can. Our inability to track him down is because he's oblivious to what happened and must be involved in some pet project that requires him and his wife being away from home and incommunicado."

Julius says, "And last night's news confirms what you just said, Richie, but I'll hold off on that 'til we finish talking about the bigger issue here."

Mick says, "That Eli may of been clueless about what Red done, but that ain't change the fact that that dipshit shudda taken better care of Al's computer. When somebody does you a solid, like Al done for that screwball Eli, trustin' his computer to him, Eli's supposed to guard it with his life. You ain't just walk away from it and let any bum who walks by do whatever the fuck they want with it. We may not need him right now, but that shithead ain't off no hook."

I say, "Okay, well said, Mick, but Richie and Mick, you too Julius, you all think that we should just maintain the status quo and ride out the storm? That plan doesn't sit well with me at all."

Richie says, "No, not at all, Al. While we don't know who this 'George' is, we do know that what happened was orchestrated by some third party who's engaged in cyber-criminal activity. Now, I have a number of clients in the same field of criminal endeavor. I'll start to shake some trees and see what results."

Mick says, "And, yeah, I'll do the same with folks I know. Youse'll see somethin'll come outa this. And, again, we gotta stay hush-hush about Red. Don't want him to blab all over the place, the same like I say before about no publicity or 'em *disgraziats* who stole your money'll disappear. And, like I already tole you Al, if that greedy no-good bastard Red finds out that the easy money job he done ended up gettin' this George almost two mill, he'll go broadcastin' his bitch about bein' bamboozled to the ends of the earth, and I'll hafta get Dominic to go back to his old occupation to shut that fuck up."

Julius says, "And I'll see what I hear from folks I know in the hacker community."

I say, "But won't all your inquiries stir the pot, so to speak, and get everyone talking, and we risk word eventually getting to the culprits?"

Richie says, "That's a good point, Al, but Mick, Julius and I know how to conduct this sort of inquiry in a discreet manner, so it's unlikely that the responsible folks will get wind of what we're up to.

"But I have to say this was some unfortunate coincidence that happened. You know, that Red should chose to do his thing on the very day that Eli happened to have borrowed your computer, Al. We don't know which of Mick's attorney cousins was the target, whether you, Al, or Eli. And based on what Mick said about Red's inability to remember names and to keep names straight, our crooks may have thought they were getting to Al in the first place, and it was Al's misfortune that they were able to achieve that goal in the roundabout manner in which they did.

"Sorry, I'm running late for court and need to get going. This is to be continued. But I'm really curious about the news piece from last night's news that you referred to earlier, Julius. I'll catch up with you about that later."

Mick says, "Before you run off, Richie, let me get this thing that's botherin' me offa my chest. Al, doncha fuckin' think that alla this gets pinned on stupid Eli. None of this money'd disappeared if only you, my imbecile asshole cousin, had half a brain and ain't let my other dipshit cousin, Eli, take your computer outa your office. This whole *budell* ain't wudda happened if you say to moron Eli, 'I'll do you the solid you ask, but only if you use it here.' So friggin' simple.

"Eli ain't could do that 'cause the files for the thing he gotta write and then send to the court by computer are at D'Amato's? That's total bullshit. All that asshole hadda do is take a few blocks' stroll to D'Amato's and brin' 'em files here. How fuckin' hard's that? And this little exercise wudda done fat Eli some good. That little effort wudda avoided all the time and effort we wasted so far and who the fuck knows how much more time and effort we gotta waste, 'cause Al here's such a lousy patsy and ain't put his foot down when he hadda. And who the fuck knows if after all we do, we gonna be able to fix this shit and get that stolen dough back. And we ain't talkin' a few dollars and cents. We got almost two mill at play here. And Mary and little Roger's future too, I hope youse ain't forgot.

"Okay, I said my piece, got that offa my chest. You could get goin' Richie."

I could have cried.

CHAPTER 18

"Parking Spot Zorro."

"**That news thing** Julius was talkin' about just might be the 'somethin' very important' moron Eli's talkin' about in that grave email he sent you, Al."

"Grave email? Oh, you mean what I said was Eli's cryptic email.

"Mick, like I tried to explain to you, cryptic has nothing to do with death or burial, it means something that's ambiguous."

"There you go again, usin' 'em big, high falutin' words with me, makin' sure you show me how dumb I am."

"Mick, don't get started."

"Fuck you. You so friggin' smart, how you explain this stinkin' mess you in the middle of, wastin' my time, and Richie's and Julius's time tryin' to fix it for you."

"Sorry, Mick. Let's get this back on track, please.

"What do you mean about the news thing that Julius referred to?"

"It's got somethin' to do with one of the millions of things that asshole Eli bitches and carries on about."

"Which is?"

"How the city's takin' away parkin' spaces."

"Okay, we all complain about the dearth of parking spaces here in Downtown Brooklyn, what with all the new construction, with over ten thousand new apartments and thousands of new residents and lots of additional cars. And most of these high-rise buildings are going up on what used to be off-street parking lots and parking garages. I very much doubt that the off-street parking in the new buildings equal the lost off-street spots, and I know it costs more to park in the new spots."

Mick says, "Yeah, some guy in the know tells me that the knuckleheads who decide how many spots the new buildin's hafta have got their heads up their butts and think that people ain't gonna be usin' cars no more. Those idiots think bikes and car sharin' are the thing of the future. What a load of crap."

"And a lot of on-street spots have been lost to accommodate CitiBikes and are reserved for car-sharing vehicles."

"And then there's 'em no parkin' signs that ain't belong where they're put, and there's also 'em yellow and white stripes they put on the street that say you ain't could park over 'em. Eli mouths off big that 'em friggin' things're only there to drive folks like us outa our fuckin' minds. Says they ain't serve no legit purpose. Ain't could say I ain't couldn't agree with him more, to tell you the God-honest truth.

"Anyways, I watched the thing on last night's news that Julius was talkin' about and it makes me think that that *strunz* Eli finally lost it and went and done somethin' about this parkin' bullshit."

"What are you talking about, Mick? Sure, I heard Eli's rants. And as you said you've also bitched about how much harder it is to find a parking spot these days. I've complained about that too. Lots of time during the day it takes me an hour to find a spot, even a metered spot.

"But Eli wouldn't dare actually act on his gripes? Even you with your balls of steel wouldn't do that. No one would want to get caught tampering with signs or painting over those stripes."

"Well, I got to the office after our meetin', and Julius tells me if you go to the Channel 2 news' website and search for the news bit they call 'Parkin' Spot Zorro,' you'll see what I'm tellin' you."

I typed in the website address for the local news station of a national network.

"Okay, the page is open. Which news segment?"

"Click on the thing near where it says 'Parkin' Spot Zorro.' It's right over there to the right."

I do as Mick directs. The video shows a man with a hard hat, protective goggles, and a construction vest with DOT on it. The newscaster says it's after midnight. The fellow is on a ladder that's being held by some woman, who also is wearing a hard hat, protective goggles, and similar vest. The man's protective goggles appear to be over regular eyeglasses.

"Hey, that's in front of the old Ex-Lax building, on the north side of Atlantic between Bond and Nevins. Must have been converted from the factory where they made laxatives to a housing co-op something like forty years ago. There are 'No Parking' signs that cover a stretch in front of the building that could accommodate four or five parked cars. There's no discernable reason why parking should be prohibited there. I've been ticketed for parking there even after paying the meter and before my time expired. Only then did I notice the No Parking sign. Since then, I've seen cars get towed from that stretch."

"Yeah, my good buddy Carmine Morielli bitched to the Community Board, and 'em bozos tell him Department of Transportation's records show that the no parkin' is 'cause those spaces supposed to be a loadin' zone. Of course, that's news to everybody and a bunch of jive-ass bullshit. Ain't loadin' zones got signs that say 'No Parkin' Loadin' Zone'? The signs there just say 'No Parkin' period; nuttin' about loadin'. There ain't been no loadin' zone there since it's been an apartment buildin'. So, those fuckin' No Parkin' signs ain't should be there. No question about it.

"If the Community Board and Department of Transportation folks opened their eyes, they'd see 'em No Parkin' signs ain't belong there. 'Em assholes so fulla shit, they could use tons of the stuff that that there closed Ex-Lax factory usta make.

"And I get friggin' sick when I hear that jive about 'If youse see somethin', say somethin'.' I drive around the city, just like all 'em city workers, cops, firefighters, sanitation workers, even high rankin' officials, alla 'em, and they all see the same shit that needs to be fixed that I see, and ain't nobody says shit and nuttin' gets done. And when somebody, like my pal Carmine Morielli, says somethin', they spit some bullshit excuse in your face. I know lots of 'em folk that work for the city, loads of 'em are friends, and a number of 'em are great folks, but I gotta say that there are too many of 'em folks that work for the city that get paid to give a shit and ain't give two shits about nuttin', 'cept gettin' paid, laid, retired and live off the tit of those of us too stupid to not know how not to pay no taxes.

"But shit, let's watch this news report."

The newscaster mentions the video is put together from both NYPD surveillance cameras as well as cameras from nearby buildings.

I watch the man climb the ladder placed against a light pole and use some sort of metal cutter to cut through the metal supports of a "No Parking Anytime" sign. After the man hands the sign down to his woman assistant, she hands him what looks like a magic marker, and he uses it to add an arrow point to the two-hour parking sign that's below the sign he removed. This change extends the two-hour parking zone to the previous no parking zone governed by the removed sign. The guy then goes with the ladder and his assistant to the pole with the No Parking sign on the other end of the no-parking zone and repeats what he had done on the opposite pole. He completely eliminates the former no-parking zone and extends the two-hour metered parking zone.

"You see that?" say Mick. "Recognize the asshole on that ladder? How about his lady partner?"

"No. I have no clue who they are. First of all, Eli doesn't have much hair and there's a stock of curly hair flowing out of that guy's hard hat."

"Ever hear of a wig? Look close. That idiot gotta be none other than my crazy-ass cousin Eli. And that lady's gotta be his wife Lucy, who looks like she's finally lost her marbles."

The rest of the news clip shows this man and woman go over to the yellow no-parking striped area near the southwest corner of Bond and Atlantic, scrape off the burnt-on plastic stripes, and paint over the area in a grayish color that matches the street color. The formerly striped-over area is now legal to park on.

The newscaster reports that this team is also suspected of altering posted signs that resulted in reversing the north-to-south orientation of traffic flow on the block of Bond Street between Livingston and Schermerhorn Streets, returning the flow to its previous south-to-north orientation, a change made about a year ago. Many in the neighborhood (including Mick, Eli and me) railed against it, as it resulted in diverting traffic to more heavily congested options to get to the BQE ramp on Tillary Street and to the Manhattan Bridge.

I say, "You know, Mick, assuming you're right that this is Eli and Lucy, this truly just may be the 'something very important' that Eli mentions in that email, and which may also be the 'matter of civic importance' he mentioned to me on the day he borrowed my computer. If it is, then he certainly must lay low. You heard the newscaster report that the police and DOT say a full-scale investigation is underway to identify and arrest the persons responsible for these actions and to prosecute them to the fullest extent of the law—whatever that's supposed to mean."

Mick says, "Yep, they're on the trail of the Parkin' Spot Zorro, like they says. Well, I guess we ain't no longer gotta give a shit about where that airhead might be, since there ain't any info we need from him. But I'm still pissed at you, like you know, and gotta bop that Eli good when he finally shows his ugly mug for not gettin' back to us right away. We wasted lots of time and energy tryin' to track that screwball down."

CHAPTER 19

"An uphill battle."

"FOR THE LIFE OF ME, I do not know how you intend to establish your client's innocence without any credible witnesses to back up the story you just told me. It's going to be an uphill battle for you to convince the Committee not to discipline Mr. Forte."

Patrick McCormack said this to Richie and me during a prehearing conference among the three of us. Mr. McCormack is the Deputy Chief Counsel of the Grievance Committee for attorneys practicing in Kings County, which is coterminous with Brooklyn. The Rules for Attorney Disciplinary Matters permit the Committee's Chief Counsel to require any attorney who is the subject of a grievance complaint and facing potential discipline to attend an informal prehearing conference in anticipation of a hearing before a panel of the Grievance Committee. Richie advised me that the conference will permit us to screen my side of the story regarding the matters that resulted in a complaint being lodged against me *sua sponte* ("on its own initiative") by the Committee based on what it heard from Charter Bank. That complaint, if decided to be valid, could result in my being either privately admonished, censured (publicly scolded), suspended from practicing law for a period of time, or even disbarred and stripped of my law license. Contesting the complaint is, therefore, something that requires my utmost attention.

McCormack says, "The Committee's concern is the disappearance of the escrowed funds. We are already aware of instances of attorneys who have themselves arranged for their escrow accounts to be raided, either by themselves or through accomplices hacking a bank's online or similar electronic platform or by their or their accomplices' pulling it off by orchestrating what appears to be an act of identity theft. In either case, the intent is to pocket those funds and to further recoup the stolen monies from the victimized bank.

"Charter Bank informs us that, in Forte's instance, its cyber investigators determined that the computer that raided his escrow accounts is the same computer he used to set up online banking for his various accounts and which performed online banking for those accounts over time. This determination was made by comparing the identifying features—his computer's fingerprints, so to speak—of the computer used in each and every instance, including the alleged theft, and finding that they are identical. I believe you are aware of this determination."

Richie says, "Yes, we are."

"So, you will need to counter this determination by Charter Bank's investigators in order to avoid the Committee's finding probable cause that Mr. Forte engaged in professional misconduct warranting the imposition of public discipline. If that finding is reached, then the Committee will authorize formal disciplinary proceedings before the Appellate Division. I assume you have some explanation of what happened."

Richie tells McCormack about Eli's borrowing of my computer and working with it at D'Amato's. Richie also reports that the waitress Iris Marchetti says she witnessed someone removing some gadget from my computer and how we learned from that person—without identifying Red—that he had stuck something into the computer thinking that he was only retrieving valuable attorney computer programs. Finally, Richie relates Julius's "expert opinion" that there are programs and devices capable of not only copying a computer's files, but also its identifying credentials, and that based on what we learned from Iris and the unidentified person, this is likely how some cybercriminals were able to make it look like it was me who raided my personal, business and escrow accounts using what looked like my computer, but which was instead a clone of my computer.

McCormick says, "Well, I will be upfront with you. As not all complaints warrant a formal hearing in front of the Committee, the Committee's Chair Gail Rubin informed Chief Counsel Thomas Hope, my boss, that your client's certainly does. And, given the theft of escrowed funds, Mr. Forte's complaint will be heard on an expedited scheduling basis. So, it is imperative that your witnesses be available to testify at the hearing when it is called. And expect to get a hearing date in the next day or two for a hearing to occur within seven days or so from when you are notified."

I shudder to hear this.

Richie says, "I do not understand why you are rushing to judgment on this. Al has a sterling reputation and has done nothing that would justify anyone to imagine he could possibly be behind the theft of those funds. And don't forget that his own personal and business accounts were also stolen, and he lost substantial sums himself."

McCormack says, "That will be considered. But we have seen attorneys who are longstanding pillars of the community take a sudden turn and engage in the most disgraceful criminal behavior. And to be blunt, the theft of Mr. Forte's personal and business funds may be considered by the Committee as not having any exculpatory value. It may be considered to be part of a front to cover up the true underlying criminal act of robbing the escrowed monies."

Richie then informs McCormack that assembling our witnesses in short order will be problematic. He tells McCormack that Iris is quite sick, Eli cannot be found, and we cannot either reveal who used the device that stole my computer's files and its identifying information or have that person testify, because that person is not aware that his actions permitted the theft of almost two million dollars. That person only thinks valuable legal computer programs were lifted, and when that person—who's a typical wise guy—learns about the amount of money stolen, that person is sure to contact those behind the theft in order to vehemently complain about not being adequately compensated for his contribution to the theft. Richie tells McCormack the culprits will thereby know they are being sought and will take deep cover or skip town completely, frustrating the efforts to identify and bring them to justice. In lieu of that person's direct testimony, Richie offers to present a witness who will testify to what he heard that person say about what he had done to my computer.

McCormack says, "And whom may that hearsay witness be."

Richie says, "His name is Mick Forte."

"Any relation to Mr. Forte here?"

"Yes, his cousin."

McCormack rolls his eyes to Richie's response and says, "While the Committee need not adhere to the evidentiary rules that govern standard legal proceedings, it may choose to regard hearsay testimony as unreliable, for the same reasons that that type of testimony is generally inadmissible."

Richie then mentions to McCormack that our computer expert witness, Julius Ortiz, will testify. McCormack shakes his head when Richie informs him of Julius's lack of formal computer science credentials.

McCormack says, "You may be wasting everyone's time bringing a so-called expert who does not possess authenticating credentials."

It is at this juncture of the prehearing conference that McCormack makes his "uphill battle" remark. He points out that our proposed evidence in support of my innocence is "flimsy" at best and may be viewed by the Committee as "just a bunch of disrespectful jive to muck up the proceedings." He warns Richie and me that this may turn the Committee against me. This makes me realize that this mess just might get me disbarred after all is said and done.

McCormack goes on, "I must also inform you both that our phones have been ringing off the hook with calls from those whose monies were taken from Mr. Forte's escrow accounts. I am referring to parties involved with those escrows consisting of contract deposits Mr. Forte was holding for real estate transactions that have yet to close. Those funds were deposited with Mr. Forte by the buyers in those deals and the amount in each case equals ten percent of the respective purchase prices for those transactions. The buyers are concerned, of course, that they will have to pay those funds again to make up for the shortfall at the closing table. However, the sellers on those deals, and these would be your own clients, Mr. Forte, they are also calling with the concern that they may be out the amount of those deposits."

Richie then asks, "Can you tell us if your office has heard from a Mary Woodley?"

"Why? Who is she?"

"She has the most monies in escrow with Mr. Forte. Those funds have nothing to do with any real estate deal; they are part of a litigation settlement."

"That name was not among those who have called here, but now that you mention her, I see here that special escrow account he was holding for her is listed in the report Mr. Forte submitted to the Committee. Yes, quite a lot of money was stolen from her."

Richie goes on, "We're in touch with her and she is aware of what happened and, while she understandably did express displeasure with this turn of events, she has her reasons for not filing a complaint.

"In any event, allow me to cut to the chase regarding those buyers and sellers.

"Mr. Forte and I reviewed the relevant provisions of the contracts that govern the escrowed contract deposits and let me lay it out to you. There are only two straightforward provisions that are at play, and they are subparagraphs 6(b) and 6(f). Subparagraph 6(b) reads as follows, and I quote:

Escrowee shall not be liable to either party for any act or omission on its part unless taken or suffered in bad faith or in willful disregard of this Contract or involving gross negligence on the part of Escrowee.

And Subparagraph 6(f) provides as follows, and I quote again:

The party whose attorney is Escrowee shall be liable for loss of the Contract Deposit.

"So, to establish any culpability on Mr. Forte's part for the loss of the escrowed monies, a party to the particular contract has to prove that Mr. Forte either stole the money or lost it due to some extreme carelessness on his part. And our position is that neither of those is the case.

"Regarding the other provision, 6(f), as it is just about universally the case with real estate deals, the seller's attorney holds the buyer's contract deposit in escrow. So, if the escrowed funds are lost for any reason, the risk of loss would fall on those sellers, all of whom are Mr. Forte's clients.

"So, the long and short of it is that those pending deals must close, once any contingent financing is committed and any title issues are resolved. The buyers will be entitled to a credit for the contract deposit paid and escrowed, albeit subsequently stolen, and the sellers will unfortunately have to transfer title despite the fact they will be short ten percent of the agreed upon price."

McCormack says, "I am not so sure how wise it is to take a by-the-contract legalistic approach here, even if Mr. Forte is innocent and has no legal obligation to cover those losses. I am fully expecting that these parties will make their own complaints about Mr. Forte to the Committee, and any moment now. So, let me suggest you give serious thought to Mr. Forte's voluntarily making restitution for the lost escrowed funds. That would go a long way toward smoothing the waters with the Committee, and those buyers and sellers, as well as that Mary Woodley you mentioned, and anyone else I left out whose escrowed funds have also been stolen."

I glance at Richie who is ahead of the game and jumps in and says, "Restitution is not in the cards, given Mr. Forte's innocence, given that he has no legal obligation to do so— and even if he wished to do so out of the goodness of his heart, he cannot, given the amount involved and his limited resources. Besides, Mr. McCormack, you're putting the cart before the horse. There's been no word from Charter Bank about its position regarding those funds. Our dealings to date have been non-adversarial, but if push comes to shove, it's our position that Charter Bank was grossly negligent for permitting attorney escrow accounts being withdrawn by means of online banking. Charter Bank has never fully appreciated the fiduciary nature of attorney escrow accounts, and when it comes to online banking escrow accounts can be transacted no differently than your standard checking and savings accounts. There are no special safeguards to protect escrow accounts. Our position is that what happened to Mr. Forte's escrow accounts is the result of Charter Bank's lax and virtually nonexistent security measures that fail to protect such accounts."

McCormack says, "I'm sure Charter Bank does not concur with that and I would be shocked if it feels obligated to return any of the stolen escrow funds. First, it remains convinced that Mr. Forte took the money. Second, even if you prove he had no hand in taking it or in conspiring with someone else to take it, Charter Bank's alternative position is that the money disappeared because of his negligence."

Richie says, "Those positions have already been articulated to us, but only as mere possibilities. Nothing further has been communicated that Charter Bank's investigators reached any conclusions.

"Besides, the Committee should discount any of Charter Bank's allegations which attributes fault or carelessness on Mr. Forte's part. Those allegations all flow from knee-jerk suspicions of its investigators who are motivated to exonerate Charter Bank and relieve it from any obligation to return any of the stolen money, whether personal or business or escrow."

McCormack says, "Then, I guess Charter Bank has yet to serve Mr. Forte with its summons and complaint for the declaratory judgment action I am told it's bringing. It's to be brought in federal court, seeking a declaratory judgment that it has no obligation to return any of the lost money, not even Mr. Forte's personal or business funds."

Richie says, "Oh, that's screwed up, if you ask me. Those monies were lost through the acts of third-party cyber thieves who are unknown to us. And as far as I know, the FBI, informed by federally-chartered Charter Bank of what transpired, is actively conducting its own independent investigation into what happened to those monies, which means, among other things, that Charter Bank is premature with any suit and the Committee should hold off on scheduling its hearing until the FBI concludes its investigation. Once the FBI gathers and assesses its evidence from the field, the U.S. Attorney will decide whether charges are warranted, whether against Mr. Forte or, as Mr. Forte and I know, against the thief or thieves—whoever and however many they may be—who stole the monies. It is our hope and expectation that those parties will be found and prosecuted and convicted and that this all will result in the monies returned and everyone made whole. If this Committee proceeds without the benefit of the results of that investigation and of the prosecution that will follow, it cannot possibly reach a well-informed decision regarding Mr. Forte and stands to make an unfortunate mistake if it authorizes any formal disciplinary action against him."

McCormack says, "That's all well and good, but under the circumstances, and given we have heard absolutely nothing from the FBI, and it's been copied on all of Charter Bank's communications, including emails, to the Committee, the Committee will proceed full steam ahead."

Richie says, "Okay, then, I guess we're finished here. Thank you for your time, Mr. McCormack. We will get ready for that Grievance Committee hearing that you say will be scheduled shortly. Goodbye."

◆

AS WE EXIT THE Grievance Committee's offices, Richie suggests we stop off for coffee to discuss strategy some.

Richie says, "That prehearing conference, besides scaring the crap out of both of us, was nevertheless a useful exercise, as it helps to crystallize my thinking about our position.

"You know, even if it's established beyond a shadow of a doubt that a computer with the same identifying features as yours was used to carry out the thefts, there's no proof whatsoever that it was you who carried out those online banking transactions. And Julius says he can easily demonstrate how two different computers can have the same identifying features. So, those allegations will fall whether raised by Charter Bank, the Committee, or any of the parties of those deals with the lost escrowed contract deposits—and even Mary for that matter.

"Next, we hold firm to our position that your lending your computer to Eli was not gross negligence, that what happened was not foreseeable or reasonable to expect. Your computer was targeted by mysterious and exceptionally brilliant cyber thieves who pulled off this theft using that dimwit Red. This is tricky because we can't have what would otherwise be helpful testimony from Red. But, if we can get Iris to testify and with Julius's opinion, that may be enough to prevent our opponents from proving the negligence allegation that's being tossed around.

"Finally, we rely on those provisions of the contracts. One, you did nothing in bad faith and nor were you grossly negligent. Two, the contract clearly provides that the seller bears the risk of loss if the escrowed contract deposit is lost. Pretty clear, if you ask me.

"So, believe it or not, strictly legally speaking, we just may be in decent shape. Or at worst, we'll be able to give each of our opponents a run for their money and perhaps make it worth their while to settle with you, and with you at worse being publicly censured."

I say, "On one hand, I agree with you, but on the other why does it make me so uncomfortable? I get the unsettling feeling that I'm screwing these innocent folks. I was in the better position than all of them to prevent the theft from happening. They are more the innocent victims than I am."

Richie says, "You're sometimes too good to be true, Al. But don't get upset, because we are going all out to find the crooks responsible for the thefts. Only by finding them and forcing them to return the money they stole will true justice prevail for all those who are innocent, including you."

I say, "That's great, Richie, but is there any progress being made on that front? I know you are shaking trees and Mick's doing his thing, so is Julius, but at this point, after all our efforts—is there any reason to hope that we'll actually find those crooks?

"And what's up with what you said to McCormack about the FBI?"

"In truth, the FBI stuff was a bit of jive to try to back up why the Committee should not move so quick. I know some agents are talking to Charter Bank's investigators on a regular basis, but I don't know if anyone's out pounding the pavement.

"Otherwise, all I can tell you at the moment, Al, is to hold on. Right now, there is nothing solid, but we are learning a little bit more each day than we knew the day before."

"What the hell is that supposed to mean? Care to share some information to help relieve the stress that's starting to strangle me?"

"Listen, relax and get back to your day job, because going forward you'll need to be focusing almost exclusively on resolving this mess as it moves toward a climax."

"Day job? That's fast going down the toilet. My seller clients won't return my or Caroline's calls. They must be pissed at me and probably want to delay their closings until there's certainty about the contract deposits; those amounts range from as low as forty thousand to as much as three hundred thousand for one huge deal. Wherever one's situated in the range, it's a lot of money to get stiffed out of. It's such a frustrating disaster."

"What can I say?" Richie says as we head our separate ways.

Shit!

CHAPTER 20

"I'm totally overwhelmed."

"AL? THIS IS CAROLINE. Where the hell you been? I'm frantic trying to reach you. Why didn't you pick up?"

"Hi, Caroline. What's going on?"

"It's absolutely out of control over here. Calls from clients demanding their files be hand-delivered today to their new attorneys located here, there and everywhere. Calls from those clients who are selling their houses demanding that you pay the buyer's stolen deposits that you were holding in escrow. And those same seller clients, as well as the attorneys for their buyers, are badgering me to get their closings scheduled for next week.

"Then, there's been a parade of process servers, all insisting on personally serving you legal papers. These crazy guys, and a lady too, all say you must be hiding to duck them. They're driving me nuts. So, I escort each and every one of them to your office, let them check under your desk; even show them you're not in the conference room or the bathroom. Then to get them the hell out of my hair, so I can get some work done, I open every closet so they see you are not hiding there. And you should see the pile of paper that's waiting for you on your desk. Quite a stack. You better get here quick.

"Wait, hold on."

I can then hear Caroline say to someone, "Well, he's not here, and I'm not authorized to permit you to search this office. I don't care what you claim this search warrant allows you to do, I'm not letting you do anything unless you guarantee me that I will still have my job and get paid after you're finished.

"Keep your shirts on, I have my boss on the phone."

Then, Caroline says to me, "Al, those FBI agents are back and have these papers signed by a Judge Peter B. Frey that they say is a search warrant that gives them the right to search this office and take whatever has something to do with your stolen accounts. What shall I do?"

I tell her to let the agents execute the warrant. I will be there within a half hour, before they finish, and will be able to see what they propose to take.

As I rush to the office, I call Richie to inform him of this. While I'm on hold, he makes a call to our contact at the Bureau, Agent Adams, and says that Adams told him that he had tried to dissuade his colleagues from going forward with the search, but their superior is adamant that search warrants on both my office and house get issued and executed.

"My house too?" I say to Richie.

Richie says, "Apparently they'll go to your house after they finish at your office. Get to the office quickly and call me if you have an issue with anything they insist on taking. And make sure you have a thorough inventory of what they do take. You'll want to be sure that everything gets returned to you in due time."

I get to the office and see that the agents have some wire running from my computer to what must be a computer they brought to extract files and other information off of my computer. They have gathered the hard copy files with the banking statements for my office and escrow accounts, including the ledger sheets I maintain to track my active escrow accounts. Despite my protests (which Richie tells me to stifle, as the warrant gives the agents wide latitude), they also take the files for my pending closings, as well as the files for Mary's settlement of the Gilbert child support matter.

Then, after spending some time carefully scrutinizing the agents' inventory list, I escort them to my house, and after they survey the place, they decide to take only the bank statements for the personal accounts that had been raided. I do not even know where my wife keeps the statements for her various investment accounts, and they did not turn up during the agents' search. Of course, I do not volunteer that such accounts exist; Theresa would kill me if I did.

I return to the office. Caroline has calmed down. I see what she was referring to as I focus on the mound of paper on my desk. At the top is a magnum opus of a summons and complaint from Charter Bank, which retained one of the top firms to bring the declaratory judgment action that McCormack mentioned. There is also a complaint to the Grievance Committee, which appears to be made by all of the buyers and my seller clients for my pending closings with the stolen contract deposits. Then, there's another action brought by Order to Show Cause, apparently from those same buyers and my seller clients suing me in civil court.

I tell Caroline that if she hears back from any of the clients who want their files delivered by messenger to another attorney that we will be happy to do so upon the written request of the other attorney.

Then, I quickly review Charter Bank's litigation papers and the Grievance Committee complaint and the litigation papers from those buyers and seller clients and call Richie to discuss next steps.

Richie says, "God, you're getting bombarded. I don't know how we're going to handle all these fronts.

"McCormack already told us that the complaints made to the Grievance Committee are going to be heard on an expedited basis. So, we have to prioritize preparation for that.

"Regarding Charter Bank's suit, I already suggested that you retain a firm with experience handling suits involving deep-pocketed financial institutions. Now, that needs to be done sooner rather than later. You were not there to be personally served, so service of that suit has yet to be completed, but you can be sure that the steps to complete service will be done promptly, and an answer or responsive pleading must be drafted soon thereafter. Typically, the thirty-day deadline to answer or otherwise respond gets extended as a matter of courtesy between the parties' attorneys. However, the firm Charter Bank retained likes to hold its adversaries' feet to the fire, so we will need to retain defense counsel right away. Once service on you is complete and the clock starts to tick on when something is due from you to avoid a default, I will initially appear as your attorney, if necessary, and try to buy time to respond. But you need to move quickly to find and retain defense counsel, so they can get cracking on this.

"And on that front, the firm you hire will require a substantial retainer. There won't be any way around that. They'll be taking on an aggressive opponent and the issues are not cut and dry. And there will be a lot of upfront work researching the issues and devising appropriate strategy. I will help you, but a decision needs to be made right away, and you need to call Mick today about whether he will fund the retainer. Let him know as gently as you can that it may be as much as $50,000."

"That much upfront?"

"Yes, sir, and pray it isn't more."

"Geez. Okay, I'll call him once I get off the phone with you.

"Now, Richie, in both the complaint to the Grievance Committee and the litigation by those buyers and sellers, they first and foremost demand that I personally fund the stolen contract deposits or, alternatively, that I be replaced by another attorney who will close those deals, but with the parties' rights being reserved to sue me post-closing with respect to those contract deposits. That litigation's Order to Show Cause demands we state why that relief should not be granted when the Order's scheduled to be heard in two weeks."

Richie says, "You'll send me a copy of all those papers later, but do you have an issue with agreeing to close those deals right away with the buyers and sellers being able to sue you later regarding the lost escrows?"

"I really don't have an issue with that, as long as they agree that subparagraphs 6(b) and 6(f) that we discussed with McCormack earlier survive and would be what we would be fighting about. That seems reasonable. Besides, I would hope and pray that soon, one way or the other, through the strings you and Mick and Julius are pulling, we recoup those monies, and the sellers would be made whole."

"Yeah, start lighting those candles each time you pass a church. But in any event, once those real estate deals are closed, that takes some pressure off. But don't expect to collect any legal fees from those seller clients of yours. You'll have to forgo your fee, and it'll get applied to the amount each of those sellers are being shorted."

"But if we do recoup the escrowed funds, then I draw my fees from the contract deposits."

"Yes. If we're so lucky."

"Richie, your pessimism is not helping."

"Sorry, Al. I know it must be overwhelming for you."

"Overwhelming. No, I'm totally overwhelmed, that's what I am."

"Anyway, who's the attorney on that Order to Show Cause? I'll contact him and see if we can stipulate to what you and I just discussed and avoid wasting time in court."

"The attorney who brought that action and who also assisted these folks with their complaint to the Grievance Committee is a David Mazza. You know him?

"I know of him but wait, you're saying he assisted those buyers and your seller clients to both file the complaint with the Grievance Committee and to bring that case brought on by that Order to Show Cause?"

"Yes."

"Is he one of the buyers' attorney?"

"No."

"Then, how could he know anything about these people's transactions, the lost escrows, and how to contact them?"

"I don't know. It's possible he knows one of the buyers or one or more of their attorneys.

"But, then, even if he happens to know any of them, how could he know the other buyers and all the sellers?"

"Yeah, and the buyers and their attorneys and, my client sellers too, are scattered all over the place. Several are from around there, a couple from different parts of Brooklyn, and the others from Manhattan, Staten Island, Westchester and Long Island."

Richie says, "Are copies of those deals' contracts in your electronic files?"

"Yes. Francesca scans all of the signed contracts and saves them in our electronic files. And she organized those files such that the pending sales and pending purchases have their separate subfolders within a pending closings folder. As each deal closes, its subfolder gets moved into a closed transactions folder. Makes it very easy for me to find stuff."

Richie says, "And the way she's organized your files would also simplify a stranger's sorting out your pending real estate transactions if she or he had access to your electronic files?"

"Yes, that's right. And each contract includes the parties' contact information."

"I wonder how Mazza got to know about those deals, the stolen contract deposits, and how he was able to reach each of those buyers and sellers and get them to retain him to bring that complaint and to start that lawsuit.

"Did he get those folks' contact info from your electronic files? Could he be the mastermind behind raiding your computer and taking that money? Or was that information provided to Mazza by those behind stealing your money, working in cahoots with him?

"It's also possible—and probably more likely—that Mazza has an inside source at the Grievance Committee who's aware of the complaints brought before the Committee and alerts Mazza of potential opportunities that may result in nice legal fees for Mazza, in return for a suitable kickback to the insider at the Grievance Committee, of course. That report you filed with the Committee discloses all of those parties and their contact info. I can't imagine it'd be terribly difficult for Mazza to get his hands on that."

"But, Richie, you say you know of Mazza. What do you know about him?"

"Yeah. He's young, thirty-something and a hot shot from Bensonhurst who shares space in an office on Court Street. Handles mostly criminal defense for lots of wise guys and other hoods. Said to be somewhat shady himself. You know they say: You start hanging around criminals long enough, you start acting like them. I think I've managed to avoid that, but the little I know about Mazza, I'm not so sure he resisted that occupational hazard of criminal defense attorneys.

"And given the way that that kind of attorney operates, it wouldn't surprise me at all if he's the type who doesn't wait around for clients to come to him, but who goes out and hustles up business. That just may be how he got those folks to retain him. If so, it's sleazy, but it's not worth wasting any time speculating about. We need to focus on preparing for the Grievance Committee hearing and our response to those pending lawsuits by Charter Bank and those buyers and sellers.

"But, let's say for the sake of argument that stealing the money was only part of a larger scheme to thoroughly fuck you. If that's the case, wouldn't the list of suspects be a short one? Who could possibly have a vendetta against you of all people, as fair as you are?"

"I really don't have any enemies, Richie. There's Gilbert, of course, but he's put away and would be hard pressed to engineer from prison something as elaborate as what's happening to me.

"You know, Mary Woodley had raised the possibility of Gilbert's involvement, but I dismissed it. I told her it'd be unproductive to give that possibility serious thought. Besides his being locked up, don't you recall how defeated and dejected he was when he was arrested and got sentenced?"

"I sure do, Al. And I know how getting jailed breaks a person, and Gilbert walked into the joint already a broken man. As I laid it out to you when you were in the can, the experience there is not uplifting, not even at a cozy federal pen, like Danbury where Gilbert's doing his time. If, on the other hand, Gilbert had gone in defiantly, it'd be different, and we'd have good reason to suspect him based on what we know. But we can dismiss that as a possibility. Otherwise, we'd only be spinning our wheels, and at this juncture we do not have time to speculate on mere theoretical scenarios."

"But not having any clue as to who has it in for me is disturbing and keeps me up at night."

"Well, hang in there, Al. Among Mick, Julius and me, something is sure to come to light before too long."

"Thanks, Richie, I guess that's my only hope at the moment."

In this time of despair, the only true source of reassurance came from an email from Mary Woodley, the person who has the most to lose unless this fiasco gets resolved. She apologized for what she characterized as her "nastiness" the last time we spoke. She wrote that upon reflection she has every confidence that I will recoup her money.

This helps to alleviate some of the guilt I feel from Mary's initial reaction. On the other hand, I also realize how much guiltier I will feel should I ultimately fail her and her son Roger.

CHAPTER 21

"A risk he refuses to accept."

"**Good morning, Al.** Heard from Patrick McCormack of the Grievance Committee."

"Morning, Richie. What did he have to say?"

"The hearing is scheduled for a week from today. We are the only hearing on its afternoon calendar. We have to be there with all of our witnesses by 2 p.m. And it's going to be a consolidated hearing."

"Consolidated? You mean both the Committee's *sua sponte* complaint and the complaint of the buyers and my seller clients?"

"That's right."

"But we only received that second complaint yesterday."

"Correct. Of course, I made that point to McCormack. But he tells me the Committee's Chief Counsel Thomas Hope says since the underlying facts and complaint are identical, there's no reason for the Committee to conduct two separate hearings. Says, too, that those missing escrowed contract deposits warrant the complaint of those buyers and your seller clients being given a particularly expedited preference. You said each of those deals are ready to close, right?"

"Yes. The deals with financing have bank commitments in place and any title issues are resolved. We are ready to close them all, but, God, I'm so nervous. Wish we had more time.

What if nothing meaningful comes to light by next week's hearing that could help us find who's behind this?"

"I agree, Al. Worse comes to worst, we'll have to apply for a new hearing based on new evidence. I hear Thomas Hope is a stickler, but he's also known to be fair and reasonable. Nevertheless, let's pray for a miracle between now and the start of the hearing.

"Anyway, David Mazza returned my call from yesterday. And he's a piece of work. Mick would call him a piece of shit and would be a hundred percent correct."

"But did he agree to stipulate as we discussed?"

"No, he vehemently opposes it. And you want to know why?"

"Of course, I do."

"He says and I quote, 'If we resolve the Order by a stip outside of court, how can I justify the fees my clients are paying me.' The twerp goes on to say, 'I have to put on a show in front of them in court, so they feel they're getting their money's worth.' He's nothing but a friggin' showboat."

"That's what it sounds like."

"He also claims that the Feds are going to be at the Grievance Committee hearing next week and said he wouldn't be surprised if they take you into custody after he gets through with you."

"Is that so about the FBI being there, Richie?"

"I'll find out from Adams if any FBI agents will attend, but I doubt very much they'd arrest you if any are present. They have no grounds. Mazza's blowing smoke, you ask me. Trying to impress me on what a tough adversary we're up against. The only semi-legit point he raised against the stip is how to address unforeseen contingencies, like your getting arrested and not available to do those closings. I pointed out that with some thoughtful drafting the stip could contemplate that possibility and any others we think of, but he said forget about it. So, there's no way around the court hearing in two weeks on the Order to Show Cause that Mazza brought in civil court.

"Anyway, you talk to Mick about the retainer for the firm to defend you in Charter Bank's lawsuit?"

"I sure did, and he told me to go fuck myself, that he's not paying good money after bad. He tells me he spoke with Mary and agreed to front the tuition deposit she needs to pay to resume her doctoral program. He considers that to be part of his loan to me that will be repaid if and when the stolen money is ever returned. He says, slim as it is, there is some chance for that to happen. But he says the retainer is spent and gone once it's paid without any similar source to cover it. So, in that case, I would somehow, some day, have to repay that to him. And that, he tells me, is a risk he refuses to accept. So, I don't know what to do on that front."

Richie says, "Well, service on you still has yet to be completed, so that clock isn't ticking yet. Let's take this a step at a time. Focus now on preparing for the Grievance Committee hearing next week. Once you do get served in Charter Bank's action, I'll give Mick a call and perhaps by then he will have softened up some. So, let that hang for the time being.

"Did Mick have anything else to say? I haven't spoken with him since the day before yesterday."

"Oh, yeah, he said that something prompted him to call Lucy's work phone. She must have changed the message remotely, because Mick says that her message now says that she's on an extended vacation and is due back at her desk the week after next."

Richie says, "So, she and Eli must have had that vacation scheduled for right after they pulled that Parking Spot Zorro action in order to disappear for a while.

"That's not going to prevent Eli from getting an earful from Mick, and from me and you too, once he's back."

I say, "Yep. Mick tells me, 'That scumbag Eli's gonna have hell to pay.'"

"Okay, let's meet tomorrow to prepare for next week's Grievance Committee hearing."

CHAPTER 22

"We are here for The Matter of Al Forte."

HERE IS THE OFFICIAL transcript of the hearing before the Grievance Committee for the County of Kings, of the Second Judicial Department of the State of New York for The Matter of Al Forte, conducted at the Committee's official hearing room:

RUBIN: "Good afternoon, all. Please settle down, so this hearing may commence.

"I am Gail Rubin, Chair of the Grievance Committee for the County of Kings, of the Second Judicial Department of the State of New York. The others sitting on either side of me are six members of the Grievance Committee who with me are conducting this hearing. We will be assisted in this task by our Chief Counsel, Thomas Hope, and his Deputy, Patrick McCormack, who are seated behind us.

"I now give the floor to Chief Counsel Hope, for him to set the stage for this hearing."

HOPE: "Thank you, Chairperson Rubin. I would characterize what will transpire here over the next hour or so as a semiformal hearing.

"As you can see, a stenographer is here who will transcribe all that is spoken during this hearing to produce a record of it. And for the record, I hereby note this hearing's start time of 2:05 p.m.

"We are here for The Matter of Al Forte. The respondent, Al Forte, was admitted to the practice of law in the State of New York by the Second Judicial Department under the name Alphonsus Salvatore Forte. At all times relevant to this hearing, the respondent maintained a registered address within the Second Judicial Department.

"This is a confidential hearing. Generally, only the respondent, the complainants, and their respective attorneys and witnesses are permitted to be present at a hearing of this Committee. Representatives of law enforcement agencies with jurisdiction over the matter at hand are also permitted to be present.

"As you entered this room, each of you signed the attendance sheet which notes at the top that by your signing it, you agree not to disclose to anyone what occurs during this hearing under the penalties that govern this hearing, which include the possibility of monetary fines and in the appropriate case even imprisonment. So, if anyone cannot abide by this, now is the time to take your leave.

"I note for the record that no one has left.

"There are two complaints that have been filed against Mr. Forte. The first was filed by this Committee itself, on its own initiative. S*ua sponte* are the Latin words for that term that we lawyers use. This Committee's complaint is in response to information received from Charter Bank, which reported to us that each and every escrow account maintained by Mr. Forte at that bank was emptied by online transfers to an untraceable offshore account. Charter Bank informed us that the transfers were initiated by the same computer that established online banking for those accounts and which had conducted standard online transactions over time. It has been confirmed by investigators that the computer used to transact those online transactions to be Mr. Forte's computer. Charter Bank further notified us that it had experienced a number of instances where certain other attorneys themselves had emptied out their escrow accounts claiming that it has been done by hackers or by someone who had stolen their identities, for the purpose of stealing the money and enriching themselves.

"The Committee's complaint alleges that Mr. Forte stealthily transferred those escrow funds and then made a false claim that it was done by unknown perpetrators. The Committee's complaint also alleges that if Mr. Forte did not directly or indirectly transfer those funds, that unauthorized and unknown third parties executed those transfers enabled by gross negligence on Mr. Forte's part, which negligence being so egregious as to warrant discipline, as it reflects negatively on Mr. Forte's ability to adhere to the Code of Professional Responsibility with which all attorneys must comply.

"The second complaint was filed by parties who are on both sides of transactions involving the purchase and sale of real estate. These complainants include the buyers who contracted to buy properties from clients of Mr. Forte and who escrowed the contract deposits for those transactions with Mr. Forte. The balance of the complainants of the second complaint are those transactions' seller clients of Mr. Forte's. These complainants seek a ruling that Mr. Forte stole the escrowed contract deposits. Such a ruling, if made, would be the basis for these complainants' claims to the New York Fund for Client Protection, which would cover those losses. Those real estate transactions have yet to close.

"The New York Fund for Client Protection was also notified by Charter Bank of what occurred with Mr. Forte's escrow accounts, and this Committee and the Fund have been in close contact regarding this matter.

"We were also informed that Mr. Forte's personal and business accounts were emptied out and transferred to the same offshore account, but those accounts do not concern us.

"Guided by this State's Code of Professional Responsibility, once its investigation into this matter is concluded, this Committee will take one of the following actions:

"It may decide that Mr. Forte has not engaged in professional misconduct and is blameless.

"Or, if it finds that Mr. Forte engaged in conduct that warrants comment but no discipline, it will issue a Letter of Advisement to him.

"Or, Mr. Forte will be issued a Letter of Admonition privately disciplining him if the Committee finds that he engaged in professional misconduct that does not warrant the imposition of public discipline.

"If, on the other hand, the Committee finds there is probable cause to believe that Mr. Forte engaged in professional misconduct warranting the imposition of public discipline, to protect the public, to maintain the integrity and honor of the legal profession, and to serve as a deterrence to others, it will authorize a formal disciplinary proceeding and turn the matter over to the Appellate Division for a panel of that court's judges to decide on the appropriate discipline, if that court, in fact, concurs that this Committee's findings warrant public discipline. If that court does concur, then Mr. Forte will be either (i) issued a public censure or (ii) be suspended from practicing law for a set period of time or (iii) disbarred which will prevent him from practicing law forever, unless his license is later reinstated upon application to and approval by the Appellate Division. And let me assure you that the law license of a disbarred attorney gets reinstated very rarely, and in order for that to happen the applicant must satisfy a veritable gauntlet of extremely difficult questions to satisfy the Appellate Division that, among other things, she or he has been fully rehabilitated and has done right by those who were harmed by the actions which resulted in the applicant's being disbarred.

"Before we commence the actual hearing, my Deputy, Patrick McCormack, indicated to me that he needs to clarify the presence of a particular person."

McCORMACK: "Thank you, Chief Counsel Hope. I note that the capacity of each person in attendance here is clearly noted on the attendance sheet with one exception. Would Mr. Gregor Weissman please inform us of his connection with this hearing? Is he a witness?"

MAZZA: "Excuse me, I am David Mazza, attorney for the complainants who filed the second complaint against Mr. Forte. Sitting next to me is Gregor Weissman, who is my assistant."

McCORMACK: "Very well, sir. Just note that you as an attorney are responsible to oversee the acts of your nonlawyer employees. So, particularly with respect to the obligation to maintain the confidentiality of this hearing, should Mr. Weissman violate that obligation there may be circumstances where you, Mr. Mazza, may be subject to discipline."

MAZZA: "Thank you, sir. I am well aware of that and I won't be losing any sleep over it."

McCORMACK: "Okay. One last thing, I was asked to point out that there are several special agents of the Federal Bureau of Investigation present here. As Charter Bank is a federally chartered financial institution, the alleged crimes committed by the unauthorized removal of the escrow funds from Mr. Forte's escrow accounts violate federal statutes over which the FBI has jurisdiction to investigate and enforce. That's the reason for those agents' presence at this hearing. Otherwise, the office of the District Attorney and the NYPD would be the law enforcement agencies represented here."

(Richie whispers to me, "Told you that you had nothing to worry about the feds being here. Don't you see Adams's here too. He'd tell me if they were going to arrest you.")

RUBIN: "Now that the preliminaries are over, let's get this hearing underway."

MAZZA: "Excuse me please, but I would like each of my client complainants to give testimony."

HOPE: "What exactly would they testify about? We already have copies of their contracts and of the checks the buyers used to pay the contract deposits. They were provided by Mr. Forte and he has not questioned the payments of those deposits or the amounts paid."

ABBATELLO: "That is correct."

MAZZA: "That's well and good, but I want this Committee to hear the burden that the loss of those monies would be for these folks."

(Richie whispers, "He's getting ready to put on a show for his clients. Watch him sing and dance.")

RUBIN: "Chief Counsel Hope will correct me if I am wrong, but the mere fact of the loss is what concerns this Committee. Whether or not it renders a person penniless may be an issue if culpability is ever established on Mr. Forte's part. For if he stole money from a poor person or if he committed a theft which renders a party poverty-stricken, that would be considered in deciding the severity of the appropriate discipline. That is not an issue at this stage."

McCORMACK: "Allow me to confirm that that is correct. Also, I reviewed the contracts and from what I see, none of the buyer complainants are close to being poverty-stricken, given the portion of the purchase price they are paying with cash on hand and the substantial loans they applied for. And I understand those who are financing their purchases received commitments for those substantial loan amounts. And a couple of the buyers are buying their properties on an all-cash basis. And the sellers, even if they close without collecting the respective contract deposits due to each, will all nevertheless realize substantial gains, as the Committee's investigators researched what they paid when they originally purchased the houses they are now selling."

ABBATELLO: "If I may, according to the relevant provisions of the contracts at play here, the risk of loss if anything happens to the contract deposit falls on the party whose attorney held the deposit. In this case, that's the sellers. So, those buyers are protected; at the closing, they will get a credit for the amount of the contract deposit each paid. The sellers would be unfortunately shortchanged that amount.

"And permit me to add that where the law draws the line oftentimes does not result in conclusions that are fair to all. That simply is the harsh reality we are all faced with at times."

MAZZA: "So, from what I hear, this says to me that Mr. Forte is refusing to do the right thing by his very own clients and is happy to just let them walk from the closing table shorthanded.

(Richie whispers: "The fucker's stirring up the pot.")

"In light of that, let me urge the Committee to give serious consideration to the following remedies which the Rules provide:

"One, the Committee move the court for Forte's immediate interim suspension,

"Two, the Committee appoint another attorney to close these transactions for the seller complainants, who are Forte's clients, and

"Three, pursuant to Judiciary Law §90(6-a), Forte be required to make restitution to these folks, so they are made whole and the Client Protection Fund need not advance a penny for his thievery.

"I do not know if you are aware of this, but Forte has strong mob connections. In fact, I don't know why those FBI agents are just sitting there and not cuffing Mr. Forte and taking him away."

(Richie whispers to me, "If it wasn't for that jerk's own mob connections, he'd be dispensing Italian ice for a living on the corner of 18th Avenue and 86th Street.")

ABBATELLO: "I object to every single word Mr. Mazza just spoke."

HOPE: "Mr. Mazza, please, this hearing is just beginning, and you want us to jump to conclusions even before we start. Sit back and let's listen to the testimony being offered on Mr. Forte's behalf."

MAZZA: "I beg your indulgence to make one additional important point."

HOPE: "All right, but please make it quick."

MAZZA: "Thank you.

"The Committee must make additional note of Mr. Forte's failure to advise his clients, the complainants who are the sellers in those deals where the contract deposits went up in smoke, of the ramifications of subparagraph 6(f) which placed the risk of loss of the contract deposits on them. They were dumbfounded to learn of this provision, and this speaks to the profound incompetence of Mr. Forte from which the Code of Professional Responsibility seeks to protect the public."

ABBATELLO: "Please allow me to address this issue."

HOPE: "Please do."

ABBATELLO: "Subparagraph 6(f) is part of the printed standard form of contract for the sale and purchase of residential properties used in the City of New York. The standard form was prepared by a committee of the bar association, and its provisions reflect the best practices for the various issues that arise in those commonplace transactions. Now, the purpose of the standard form is to avoid having to negotiate each and every one of those issues for every single transaction. Among other things, without the provisions of the standard form that reflect the considered best practices, ordinary transactions involving the sale of homes would become cumbersome, and attorneys would have to charge higher fees for those transactions. Also, a number of the issues addressed by the standard form almost never arise, and it would be a waste of time for an attorney to go over the contract form line-by-line for each and every deal. Again, it would be cumbersome and make these deals more expensive for clients.

"The issue addressed by that subdivision 6(f) rarely arises. And that is why attorneys do not usually point it out to their clients. And, so, Mr. Forte's not doing so is standard practice, not, quote-unquote, profound incompetence, as Mr. Mazza alleges."

HOPE: "Okay, Mr. Abbatello, both Mr. Mazza's and your points are on the record for this hearing and will be considered by the Committee.

"Let's move on.

"Mr. Abbatello, are your witnesses ready to testify?"

ABBATELLO: "Thank you, Chief Counsel. Allow me first to summarize what our own investigation uncovered as to how those monies were stolen from Mr. Forte's accounts, and I refer to his personal, business and escrow accounts.

"On a day when Mr. Forte would be out of his office most of the day for a real estate closing, he lent his computer to another attorney, Eli B. Ativa, who used it at a local café to prepare litigation papers. Mr. Ativa had to run out at some point, and while Mr. Forte's computer was unattended, another fellow inserted a device into Mr. Forte's computer, which copied all of his files, which included account information and passwords for his various Charter Bank accounts, as well as the identifying features of his computer. A waitress, Iris Marchetti, witnessed this fellow remove the device from the computer. That fellow who inserted the device admitted to Mr. Michelangelo Forte to his inserting some gadget into Mr. Forte's computer, thinking that it would extract valuable legal computer programs, unaware that whoever got him to insert that device would use the extracted information to steal close to two million dollars. This fellow said he thought the intent was just to sell those valuable programs. The existence of a gadget that is capable of extracting both the files and the computer's identity has been confirmed by our computer expert, Julius Ortiz. According to Mr. Ortiz, the stolen computer's identity would enable one to essentially create a clone of Mr. Forte's computer. Mr. Ortiz surmises that the money transfers at issue were transacted using said clone. Also, at the time Charter Bank states these transfers occurred, Mr. Forte was fast asleep with his turned-off computer with him in his bedroom."

RUBIN: "I do not have the attendance list before me. Please call your witnesses, Mr. Abbatello."

ABBATELLO: "Thank you, Chairperson Rubin. Unfortunately, Iris Marchetti has been dealing with mononucleosis and while she fully intended to be present at this hearing, I just received a text message from her mother that Ms. Marchetti had a relapse and is now in the emergency room of Staten Island Hospital."

HOPE: "Then how about that fellow who admitted to having inserted some device into Mr. Forte's computer? You surely produced him."

ABBATELLO: "No, I did not."

HOPE: "You could have subpoenaed him, if necessary."

ABBATELLO: "With all due respect, besides being— for want of a better word—an unreliable dimwit, we have strategic reasons for not revealing this person's identity."

HOPE: "I have to warn you that you are running the risk that your strategy just may backfire. But go on, who do you have to testify?"

ABBATELLO: "I am expecting Michelangelo Forte any minute now, sir. He had some urgent matters to attend to and should be here shortly."

MAZZA: "Mick Forte is a known hood and thug."

HOPE: "Sit down, Mr. Mazza, and restrain yourself, please.

"Mr. Abbatello, what witnesses are present ready to testify, other than your client?"

ABBATELLO: "Our computer expert, Julius Ortiz."

HOPE: "Before you call him, provide us with his credentials."

ABBATELLO: "He has no formal education in computer science or any related field of study."

HOPE: "I believe my Deputy, Mr. McCormack, at the prehearing conference informed you that we look askance at experts without recognized credentials.

"Sorry, I am not going to waste the Committee's time with the opinion of a self-taught computer geek.

"Do you have anything else to add, Mr. Abbatello?"

ABBATELLO: "Only that Mr. Forte here will swear to the veracity of my description of what we learned about what happened to his computer."

HOPE: "We will assume that is the case."

McCORMACK: "I would like to question Mr. Forte so this hearing's record more fully reflects what would have transpired had those witnesses testified."

HOPE: "Yes, please go right ahead."

McCORMACK: "Mr. Forte, please raise your right hand and tell us if you swear to respond to my questions truthfully under the penalties of perjury."

FORTE: "Yes, I do."

McCORMACK: "Thank you. First, do you concur that the statement made by your attorney, Mr. Abbatello, as being an accurate description of what you believe happened to your computer? Do not forget you are under oath."

FORTE: "Yes, I do concur with Mr. Abbatello's statement."

McCORMACK: "Now, allow me to drill down for the sake of specificity regarding certain aspects of Mr. Abbatello's statement. Did the waitress Iris Marchetti see who inserted that device in question into your computer?"

FORTE: "No, she only said she saw that fellow Mr. Abbatello mentioned remove it from my computer."

McCORMACK: "So, you don't know if that fellow or someone else inserted the device into your computer?"

FORTE: "That fellow said he had inserted the device while Eli Ativa had stepped out of the coffee shop."

McCORMACK: "Whom did that fellow tell that to?"

FORTE: "To Mick Forte."

McCORMACK: "And Mick Forte passed on this information to you?"

FORTE: "Yes."

McCORMACK: "Am I correct that you never spoke to this fellow about what he did to your computer?"

FORTE: "You are correct. In fact, I never spoke to that person in my life."

McCORMACK: "You are aware that unless we hear it out of the horse's mouth, so to speak, that it's mere hearsay, which under the rules of evidence would be inadmissible in a court proceeding. You are giving it to us third-hand. If Mick Forte told us what this mysterious fellow told him, that would be second-hand, and still hearsay."

FORTE: "Yes. You are correct."

McCORMACK: "At the hearing stage we are not so restrained, but the rules of evidence do have some bearing on the weight the Committee gives to any particular testimony.

"But let's move on. Did the waitress Iris get a good look at the device or touch it."

FORTE: "She didn't mention anything about the device to her mother."

McCORMACK: "She didn't mention anything about the device to her mother? What do you mean by that? Didn't you speak with this Iris yourself?"

FORTE: "No, Iris was too sick, and her mom passed on to me what Iris told her to tell me."

McCORMACK: "Then that's also hearsay, you know."

FORTE: "Yes, I guess so."

McCORMACK: "Regarding that attorney who borrowed your computer, what does he have to say about what happened to your computer while it was in his hands?"

FORTE: "Other than an innocuous email exchange, I have not been able to communicate with Eli Ativa since I handed my computer to him on the day he borrowed it."

McCORMACK: "You think he may behind the emptying of your accounts?"

FORTE: "No, no, not at all."

McCORMACK: "But I would think he'd be the first person you'd want to talk to."

FORTE: "I assure you that great effort's been expended trying to reach Mr. Ativa, but to no avail."

McCORMACK: "But he returned your computer. I don't suppose he just dropped it on your doorstep."

FORTE: "No, he returned it to my office. Handed it over to my assistant, and she said he just dropped it off, said thanks and left. I was out of the office at that all-day closing Mr. Abbatello mentioned."

McCORMACK: "Doesn't this Eli Ativa's disappearance give you any suspicion that he may be behind the disappearance of those monies?"

FORTE: "No. And we only just recently learned why he has been so hard to find and know it has nothing to do with what happened to my Charter Bank accounts."

McCORMACK: "Okay, let's get back to that fellow and the magic device. Did that fellow tell Mick Forte who he was working for or with?"

FORTE: "He said he couldn't recall the man's name."

McCORMACK: "If he doesn't know the man who hired him, how did he come to be hired?"

FORTE: "The fellow told Mick Forte that he was referred to that man as someone who knew how to get things done by others in the neighborhood who know him."

McCORMACK: "Did Mick Forte question him about the device or did the fellow volunteer any information about it?"

FORTE: "The answer to both questions is no. And we are certain that the fellow has no clue about the device and its capabilities."

McCORMACK: "So how did you reach the conclusion that the device had the capacity to both extract your files, as well as your computer's identifying features, thereby making it possible to create a clone of your computer?"

FORTE: "Julius Ortiz, our computer whiz, told us that such devices exist."

McCORMACK: "Does Mr. Ortiz have firsthand knowledge that the device that was inserted into your computer was such a device?"

FORTE: "No."

McCORMACK: "And was he somehow able to ascertain that such device had been inserted into your computer?"

FORTE: "He did not check my computer. So, I suppose there is no way to ascertain that."

McCORMACK: "Okay, I have no further questions."

HOPE: "Thank you, Deputy. So, it is clear that any testimony that would have been presented on Mr. Forte's behalf by those absent witnesses would have been steeped in hearsay and speculation.

(This just about shoots to shit the strong legal strategy Richie and I thought we had.)

"There is no need to waste any more of the Committee's time.

"Just let me add, Mr. Abbatello, that the shoddy nature of what's been presented on your client's behalf will not sit well with the Committee. Your next stop will likely be the Appellate Division.

(I sure could use a restroom break right now.)

"Any final words on your client's behalf, Mr. Abbatello?"

ABBATELLO: "Well, allow me to conclude with the following: No one is equipped to deal with these current cybercrimes, and no one appears to appreciate how very difficult it is to prove what happened. We continue to operate on outdated information using outdated procedures. This has become increasingly evident to me in observing how Charter Bank and this Committee are proceeding. It seems you are more willing to make Mr. Forte, who has an immaculate, unblemished record, an unwitting martyr, than do the hard work necessary to capture the elusive cybercriminals responsible for these complex and sophisticated crimes."

RUBIN: "Excuse me, but someone is knocking on the door. Would one of the FBI agents kindly see who's there?

(Agent Adams opens the door and permits a woman to enter.)

"Welcome, and please identify yourself."

STONE: "I apologize for interrupting this hearing. I am U.S. Attorney Cheryl Stone.

(Oh, I know her. Stone is the U.S. Attorney who negotiated Gilbert's plea bargain when he was arrested in connection with Mary Woodley's child support proceeding. I wonder what brings her here? I start to sweat and my heart pounds.)

"And I apologize for being late. Judge Peter Frey was tied up in a conference, which ran longer than expected.

"Anyway, I am here with arrest warrants that my FBI colleagues here will execute."

(Richie jumps up.)

ABBATELLO: "Based on what could you possibly have obtained a warrant to arrest my client? And who else besides him is being arrested?"

STONE: "Relax, Mr. Abbatello. Neither of the warrants is for your client, Mr. Forte.

(I could breathe again. But I wonder what the heck's going on?)

"The warrants are for the arrests of David Mazza and Gregor Weissman."

MAZZA: "What? What the fuck, me and Gregor?"

STONE: "You had better be quiet and let Special Agent Adams read you and Mr. Weissman your rights and cuff both of you.

"While that's being taken care of, I present to this Committee the signed confession of Gordon Gilbert, which exonerates Al Forte, the respondent of this proceeding. Mazza and Weissman are being arrested on the grounds of grand larceny, conspiracy and a variety of other crimes, cyber and otherwise."

(There is a gasp in the room, led by me.)

"Mr. Gilbert, who is presently incarcerated in the federal prison in Danbury, Connecticut, confessed under oath that David Mazza and Gregor Weissman were his accomplices and through the cyber skills of Mr. Weissman enabled the various personal, business and escrow accounts of Mr. Forte at Charter Bank to be raided and all funds extracted therefrom and transferred to untraceable accounts in a bank based in the Cayman Islands and from there further transferred to an account opened by Mr. Gilbert in a Swiss bank which has a long-standing relationship with the law firm of Adler & Stillman. Associates of mine are processing the closing of that Swiss bank account and transferring the funds back to the Charter Bank accounts of Mr. Forte from which they were stolen."

RUBIN: "Well, I guess with what just transpired we can declare this hearing adjourned.

"Chief Counsel Hope, what are next steps, please?"

HOPE: "Let me first point out to all present, and for the record, that Chairperson Rubin, Deputy Counsel McCormack, Mr. Abbatello and I were all aware of the matters of which U.S. Attorney Stone just spoke, including the pending arrests of Mr. Mazza and Mr. Weissman. We, in fact, dragged out the hearing so as to buy time for U.S. Attorney Stone to arrive with the arrest warrants so they could be executed by the FBI agents who are present. Those agents were present here for the purpose of arresting Mr. Mazza. We were not expecting Mr. Weissman to be present at this hearing, and it is a happy coincidence that he did join us.

"And to those witnessing this kind of hearing for the first time, I must confess that this is not how these hearings are typically conducted. In truth, Deputy Counsel McCormack, Mr. Abbatello and I hammed it up a bit as well to fill the time necessary for U.S. Attorney Stone to arrive with those arrest warrants and that confession.

"That being said, in conclusion please note that the complaints against Mr. Forte will remain open, but once the return of the stolen monies into those escrow accounts are confirmed by Charter Bank, the complaints will be closed, and the Committee will provide formal notice to Mr. Forte of that fact, as well as a formal declaration of the Committee's determination that there are no grounds whatsoever to discipline Mr. Forte.

"To wrap up, I hereby note for the record that this hearing adjourned at 3:17 p.m.

"Good day, all."

CHAPTER 23

"It was a thing of beauty."

"MICK, WHAT THE fuck happened? You pull the same exact crap you pulled the last time with Mary's child support case. You keep me in the dark, while you work everything out. Meanwhile, I'm stressed out of my mind, to the point of collapse.

"And frigging Richie, too, knew and says shit to me—same as the last time too. And during what proved to be that totally unnecessary Disciplinary Committee hearing, he leaves me high and dry. I'm feeling like toast, getting grilled by that Deputy Counsel McCormack asking me those silly questions. I was so humiliated and felt so horrified, convinced my career's over. And it's all just a performance, a mere waiting game to give U.S. Attorney Stone time to get the judge to sign Mazza's and Gregor's arrest warrants. For the life of me, I don't know why I had to be subjected to what I was put through. No one says crap to me, while I'm starting to look for the nearest window to jump out of. That's how terrible that hearing was, until the end, of course.

"You know, after all this, I made an appointment to see a cardiologist to make sure my heart's all right."

Thus begins my conversation with Mick when we finally get together a few days after the Disciplinary Committee hearing.

"Al, Al, what could I say? Listen, just chill out, will you?

"Okay, so it's *déjà vu* all over again. What that Brit say, all's well that ends good?"

"I'm not even bothering to correct you. Of course, I'm glad you saved the day. I got all that money back to the penny, Gilbert and Gregor and Mazza are getting their due, those buyers and sellers are happy, Mary's delighted, and I'm ready to get my practice back on track. But at what price if how you went about it takes a good ten years off my life?"

"Come on, the way Richie, Julius, JBJ, Smitty and me played it was the only way to go. We hadda keep you in the dark so those *sfaccims* could play right into our hands and hang 'emselves."

"So, how the hell did you manage to swing this?"

"Al, I gotta tell you, it was a thing of beauty, the way it played out.

"Durin' that meet I had with that shithead Red, I get this call from a strange number. I ignore it, think it's one of 'em bullshit scam calls that drive me nuts. Figure I'd check it out later once I finish with jerkoff Red.

"But then I forget all about that call, 'til I'm just about to hit the hay. And then I see that the number looks familiar, but ain't could put my finger on it, 'til it hits me, that it's one of 'em numbers for 'em burner phones we got for Mary's case. Had Julius set 'em phones up so the numbers ain't got blocked, so when a call from any of 'em come up on caller ID, we know which one of us's callin'.

"So, I listen to voice mail. It's Smitty and he says to call him at home that night or the next mornin' early before eight when he takes off for work. And tells me call him on one my burners.

"After that message, I ain't could sleep for shit. I'm wonderin' what the fuck's goin' on with Smitty?

"I'm usually out like a light soon as my head hits the pillow, but that night I'm tossin' and turnin' with all kinds a things bouncin' around in my brain. I finally fall asleep but have this strange dream about Gilbert of all the fucks on this here earth. And the bastard's laughin' his ass off about somethin'. I'm still asleep, but I'm wonderin' what the fuck'd make that *disgraziat* so happy, with his ass in the joint, even if it's a federal one?

"Woke up, hadda be about four in the mornin', still dark out. I get this real strong hunch, that I ain't could shake no matter how much I doubt it, that what happened to that dough of yours hadda been masterminded by that lowlife prick Gilbert. Somehow, someway, he pulled it off from the can.

"Decided then and there, I'm gonna see where this hunch takes me, and if I find out it does go to that fuck that I gotta backdoor it, keep it quiet, keep it especially from you, cuz, 'til it checks out. Ain't wanna get your hopes up, in case the hunch's wrong. Figure that'd really get you way down in the dumps, and I hadda protect you from that. Cudda made you suicidal, who knows?"

I say, "Appreciate your concern, Mick."

"Hey, fuck you. I ain't appreciate your snot-nose attitude. I had your best interest in mind, you asshole. Now listen and shut the fuck up unless you got somethin' useful to say.

"Anyways, I figure even if my hunch's right, you ain't got the poker face to keep this thing quiet 'til I could set up the traps I'm gonna need to set. You'd spoil the surprise that gotta be in place.

"So, when Smitty and me finally hook up, he tells me he's takin' a train, Metro North or whatever, to Danbury prison that there mornin'. He gotta take some forms for dickhead Gilbert to sign. Smitty ain't so sure what they're all about, but he smells a rat and wants to let me know. Says he's also been hearin' from this secretary at the office that she thinks somethin' bad's goin' down. Those forms hadda do with openin' some account for Gilbert with one of 'em banks in Switzerland that that law firm does lots of business with.

"Later, Smitty tells me he's shocked to see how happy shithead Gilbert is. That dick used to treat Smitty like crap, but the fucker's as nice as can be toward him. Why the fuck's that? That's what Smitty and me wondered.

"So, Smitty keeps his ear to the ground and that same secretary there says she's about to blow up, she's so pissed about some crooked shit looks like that stinkin' Gilbert's up to.

"Tells Smitty that the guy who shared the cell with Gilbert got released on one of 'em technicalities. The attorney who pulled that off's none other than that sleazo Mazza. That shyster's from Bensonhurst. Don't mean shit he's Italian. I ain't could never trust lots of 'em wops from that part of Brooklyn. That lowlife-number-one Red's from there. You see, lots more second- and third-generation Italians live there. Here, where we are, there're lots more Italians who came right off the boat, and you'll find that folks here still hold dear the traditional Italian family values.

"Anyways, hotsy-totsy Mazza gets this Gregor outa the clink. He's in there for one of 'em new cybercrimes. Looks like that guy Gregor's prince of the hackers, could pick your pocket by ticklin' a computer key or two. Later on we find out that this impresses the shit outa Gilbert. That dickhead gets the assholes who run that law firm to hire Mazza, so he can handle stuff that Gilbert needs handlin'. One of 'em things's prob'ly to see if Mazza could come up with one of 'em technicalities to get Gilbert out too. Anyways, Smitty says that this Mazza wasn't made no partner or anythin' like that. He says it was kinda some loose deal, somethin' called of counsel. But they give him an office there that he uses sometimes, and they assign him a secretary, who's the lady that's feedin' Smitty the info about Gilbert.

"So, Smitty keeps up his snoopin' and finds out that the firm has control of some of Gilbert's dough and Gilbert has 'em givin' some of it to Gregor, who visits Gilbert a coupla times. And some dough goes to Mazza too, who goes along for the ride with Gregor to see Gilbert at least once.

"I do some askin' around to get some lowdown about this Mazza and come to find out somethin' very interestin'. Guess who's the ex-hubbie of one of Mazza's mother's sisters."

I say, "I wouldn't have a clue, Mick."

"It's that fucker Red."

"Really?"

"Yep. The world's smaller than we know.

"So, this here's how this here *budell* musta got played out. Gilbert musta been impressed that Mazza got Gregor outa jail. But before Gregor got turned loose, while they're sittin' around their cell twiddlin' their thumbs, Gregor musta told Gilbert about his cyber thief skills.

"Gilbert prob'ly ain't made it no secret how much he hates your guts and'd love to fuck you over big time. He finds out Mazza's from Brooklyn, has mob contacts. Mazza knows from Red hisself or what he hears on the street that it's Red that got me in the clink, and he knows that Red operates some in this here neighborhood, and figures if Red knows me, he gotta know my cousin who's an attorney. Only, they ain't know, not even Gilbert, that I got two cousins who're attorneys.

"So they hatch a plan. They'll use Gregor's cybercrime skills, which includes how to make 'em untraceable transfers of money to offshore banks. Once the money's there, then Mazza fixes it so it all gets moved to the account they open for fucko Gilbert at that firm's friendly Swiss bank.

"They ain't know how really stupid that dimwit Red is. How he ain't good for shit rememberin' names. So, whether or not they mention your name to him, he musta hadda tell 'em he knows Mick Forte's cousin who's an attorney. Betcha he ain't even know Eli's name, and all he knows is he sees Eli at D'Amato's and that that asshole cousin of mine runs his office from there.

"I ain't surprised that they'd want Red to line up a second-story guy to get to your computer when your office's closed, but Red musta said that ain't necessary 'cause he could get to my attorney cousin's computer just about whenever he wants.

"It's your lousy luck that Red pulled off what he did on the day when Eli had your computer.

"And I betcha Gilbert just wanted to fuck you good. Had no clue and didn't give a shit one way or the other if Mary's money—his money, as far as he prob'ly thought—was still with you. He just wanted this cyber magic money-grab to revenge your draggin' his ass into the shithole he's sittin' in. He knew he'd make a real motherfuckin' mess for you withcha clients, with 'em law license folks. Figured he'd screw up your ability to work as a lawyer; who the fuck's gonna wanna hire a lawyer whose escrow money got swiped? He knows the law license folks'll be on your ass and even if you keep your license, they'd put a huge scare into you. Fuck withcha head a whole lot.

"I hear later on that that asshole Gilbert wanted to get back at me too, but Mazza told him that that'd be a major mistake that wudda backfired and screw up even what they wanted to do to you. I'm sorry they ain't tried to come after me. This wudda been lots more fun.

"And to twist the knife some more, and prob'ly to show how smart and tough he is, Mazza finds out who those buyers and sellers are on the deals where the contract deposit monies got took, contacts 'em all, and talks alla 'em into hirin' him to make that complaint to the lawyer license folks and sue you too, to make sure they pull out all 'em stops. Also happens to put a few more dollars into that greedy attorney's pocket. Looks like some of Red's greed rubbed off on Mazza, and they ain't even related by no blood.

"Meanwhile, Richie tells me he finds out from our FBI friends that they're real interested in Gregor. They're pissed that he got outa jail. They said the guy only knows how to support hisself by lettin' his fingers do the walkin' and rippin' folks off cyberwise.

"Richie and me're worried you'd be up shit's creek without a paddle unless we could somehow come up with solid proof on how your money got took. We're sure, Julius too, that whatever this Gregor got Red to shove into your computer was how they got the info about your accounts and your computer to rip you and the bank off. But the fuckin' law got all these cockamamie rules about what's good and what's bad proof.

"So, I ask Richie, what if Smitty gets us copies of those bank forms that Gilbert filled out? That help to prove what they done? We already found out that the amount of money that's bein' deposited in jerkoff Gilbert's Swiss account equals to the penny the amount of monies they took from alla your accounts at Charter Bank.

"Richie ain't was sure if that law firm'll say those copies got stolen from 'em and say that some lame excuse called attorney-client privilege would get 'em thrown outa court and not count as proof.

"So, Richie checks with that U.S. attorney who got Gilbert locked up. Richie says that when he tells her that those amounts match, she got real interested. She tells Richie she's gonna think about this and get back to him. She calls him back and says she spoke to the new boss at that law firm. Happens that guy used to be a hotshot U.S. attorney someplace else. He says to her that anythin' that had to do with doin' a crime ain't covered by that privilege excuse. He says to her he'd look into it and if what she says checks out, he'll personally deliver those forms and any other files the firm has about your money.

"I gotta say I was shocked, but copies of all 'em paperwork that show the monies goin' from some fly-by-night bank in the Caymans to Gilbert's Swiss bank account get handed over to the U.S. Attorney.

"They look it all over and go and meet with Gilbert at Danbury. They rub all this shit in his face, especially that Mary's money got took. They say to Gilbert that his plea bargain that got him only two years in the clink was 'cause he paid that money. So, 'cause he stole that dough back, he's back to square one on the original deal, and his two-year stint'll be five plus the new time for the new crimes, unless he fesses up.

"He bitches how the fuck could he know if her money's still in your escrow account. Says ain't no way they could hang that on him. Richie says they tell him, you're part of a conspiracy, so even if you ain't done shit you get hanged for whatever the others did. So, if they took Mary's money, you took her dough too.

"So, wouldn't you know it, but the asshole starts singin' like a canary. Tells 'em how he and Gregor and Mazza came up with the scheme. How they got to your computer with that gizmo that sucked all that info outa your computer. How they used your passwords to make the transfers by online bankin', yada yada yada. Gives 'em the whole friggin' nine yards.

"They put Gilbert in solitary so he ain't could get word to Gregor and Mazza. Then the U.S. Attorney and Richie, even those lawyer license folks, worked out how they'd set

Mazza up to be arrested. Nobody knows that Gregor's gonna be at that hearin', so that was like a nice surprise gift with a pretty ribbon on top.

"After all's said and done, your money's back in the accounts they got took from. Gilbert gets another two years in Danbury. Mazza and Gregor'll join him there or get their asses shipped to some other fed pens; their visits'll be for five years apiece. Mazza gotta refund the fees he collected from those buyers and sellers, and if he don't, he'll get more time added to his prison time. So, that's like a pay-to-get-out-of-jail deal."

I say, "You know, in retrospect, Mazza and Gregor had to know we were referring to Red when we spoke at the hearing about the fellow who inserted that device into my computer. I guess because nothing was said connecting Red to them, they did not react."

Mick says, "The feds were ready to jump if they did and tried to sneak out of that hearing. Those in the room were near the door to block any escape, and there were a coupla other feds right outside the room just in case. No way those punks goin' anywheres 'cept the lock-up."

"That's good and, like I said, it would have been good for me to know about all this ahead of time. In any event, it wasn't until the next day that it finally dawned on me that it was Gregor Weissman whose name Red had misremembered as George or Gregory."

Mick says, "Told you he's one dumb fuck. Anyways, Richie musta already told you that the law license folks have closed out those complaints against you, the bank stopped its lawsuit, and the feds got Mazza to sign whatever needs to be signed to cancel the lawsuit he started for those buyers and sellers. The FBI tell Richie they'll return all the stuff they took from you when they searched your office and house. And Richie says that Mazza was automatically disbarred when he pleaded guilty to the shit he pulled on you."

I say, "Yes, I am aware of all that. And I just received a letter from the president of Charter Bank apologizing for any misunderstanding and saying how proud the bank is to count me as one of its customers."

Mick says, "Well, like I said, all's well that ends good."

CHAPTER 24

The feeling is mutual.

"I TELL YOU, AL, we wrap up this *budell* real nice. Gilbert's prison vacay gets extended and that Gregor and Mazza get put away too. Then, guess which asshole I run into soon after we wrap this up, after we all went nuts lookin' all over the friggin' place for that putz?"

"Must be Eli."

"Bingo! You got it. So, I says to that joker, 'These past coupla weeks, I'm bitchin' where's that fuckin' asshole cousin of mine? Finally, you show that ugly puss of yours, after all's said and finished. And ain't you think for a second you're off the hook, you *sfaccim e med*.'

"So, I says to him, 'So, where the fuck you been hidin', Eli?'

"He says, 'Oh, here and there. I really can't say where I was or why Lucy and I had to be away and why all the secrecy. If I reveal any of that information to you, you can get into trouble; so, it's best that I leave it at that.'

"I says to him, 'However you slice it, you're an asshole. And I wanna know from you why you ain't took better care of Al's computer that time he let you borrow it? You know, you airhead bastard, why ain't you make sure nobody could screw around with it no way, while you disappear to do who the hell knows what.'

"Eli says, 'Come on, Mickie, I never secure my own computer at D'Amato's, but I did as Al directed me and secured his with the locking device he gave me, so nobody could walk away with it.'

"After yellin' at that fuckin' dipshit for callin' me Mickie, I says to him, 'Secured, my ass. Anybody lets you use any of their stuff, you take much better care of it than your own. And that means you ain't want nobody to touch it or fuck around with it in no way. You even got a file cabinet in D'Amato's storeroom, and that storeroom's off limits to everybody 'cept staff and you. Ain't could figure out why they put up with you and your shit there. You shudda turned Al's thing off and locked it in your cabinet when you went off galivantin'.'

"Before he could open his big trap, I tell him to just shut the fuck up and not say nuttin'. He ain't got no good excuses for what he done, really ain't done, withcha computer. You do him a 'solid,' and then he ain't do the right thing in return.

"Then, I says to him, 'And you make us go outa our friggin' minds tryin' to find you to see what the fuck you know about what happened, and you ain't get back to us, you lousy *disgraziat* bastard, and we find out your off doin' your crazy-ass, *pazzo* crap. Don't think we ain't know what you been up to. And you screwball even drag Lucy into your bullshit."

"He says, 'Real sorry about that, Mick, and if I knew what had happened I would have rearranged things and stayed around to help. Not knowing what happened, I needed to lay low for a while, really did.'

"Then he goes on and tells me, 'Oh, before I forget, when you see Al, besides apologizing for me about everything, do thank him. His computer was my good luck charm. I needed it to draft papers to oppose a summary judgment motion. I won and that motion was dismissed, and the other side decided it was best to settle and I got my clients big bucks and myself a nice fee.'

"I say, 'Is that right?' Well, I hear that and decide on the spot that after all the trouble that idiot put us through, I'm makin' him give me the fee he got for that case and I'm gonna split it five ways—with you, me, Richie, Julius and Smitty—so we each get paid for the time and aggravation we wasted 'cause that dope ain't took good care of your computer and then ain't could be found. This wudda been divided six ways, but JBJ who helped by settin' up that meet with Red said that gettin' Red off his aunt's back was worth more than any dough in his pocket. Told you that fella's become quite a guy."

I say, "That's great to hear about JBJ, and it's good that Eli's giving us that money."

"Before you give that dope any credit, Eli ain't exactly volunteered to do it. You might say he got his arm twisted some."

I say, "I'm not surprised, but do use my share to reimburse yourself what I owe you."

"You ain't got nuttin' to worry about there. Already plan to do exactly that. What you think? I'm gonna let you off easy? I got a rep to protect, you know."

I say, "But of course, Mick. And once Cohen figures out the balance that I owe you, I'll get that to you right away.

"And there is no amount of money which will repay the debt of gratitude I owe you for your tremendous help. Thank you very, very much for all your help and for saving my butt once again."

"I's waitin' for that *grazie*. But you know, I'm always glad to help my cuz. Next time, you gotta listen to my advice, if you wanna stay away from trouble and all kinds a bullshit that you'd avoid all together if you only listen to what I tell you."

I say, "This experience reinforces to me, once again, that I must listen to your warnings and heed your advice. Once again, I've learned an important lesson."

Mick says, "That's what you said the last time. I hope you really mean it this time. Theresa wudda chopped off your head if you ain't got this shit fixed."

"Agreed, Mick. And, incidentally, I also ran into Eli earlier today, probably after you saw him. And he did tell me he's sorry for what happened and apologized for being so hard to find.

"I asked him about the crazy stuff he was up to, and he said he was 'off living my dream.' I said to him, 'How come your dream usually turns out to be everyone else's nightmare?'"

Mick says, "You can say that again, Al.

"And later I even bump into that *skeev* Red. He starts bitchin' to me, 'I got this serious beef with you.'

"I says, 'Yeah, what beef you got with me?'

"That no-good moron then says, 'You ain't told me that that crook George or Gregory, whatever the fuck's his name, used what I done for him to score over a mill. That scumbag shortchanged me big time. My rightful piece for that job hadda be no less than a hundred G's.'

"Well, I scream at this motherfucker, 'You fuckin' shithead, almost two million bucks got robbed from my cousin. You know how much trouble and all the shit we hadda go through to fix this? We hadda deal with the FBI and my cousin almost lost his law license. Get the fuck outa my face, or I'll bash in your fat, thick skull real good this time. I ain't even give a shit if I gotta go back to jail. And you're lucky I ain't ratted you out, or you'd be in jail too.'

"That jerk then has the balls to say to me, 'Come on, Mick, I'm talkin' business here and you're takin' it all personal.'

"I says, 'You better run before I call Dominic to get here quick to do me a favor.'

"You shudda seen how fast that greedy fuck ran. He prob'ly cudda made the U.S. Olympic sprint team.

"Oh, yeah. I was in D'Amato's yesterday. Iris's back to work. Says she ain't had no mono. It was the flu and exhaustion from all the studyin' she's been doin'. Says her mom got her back to health. Guess Valerie's right that some of 'em doctors ain't know shit about what's wrong with you sometimes.

"And wait, hold on a second. Before you go, I almost forgot I got this bone to pick with you, Mr. Smarty Pants."

"What are you referring to, Mick?"

"I ain't like the way you wanted to disrespect Julius."

"Julius? What the hell are you talking about, Mick?"

"You wanna know what the fuck I'm talkin' about, you *disgraziat* lousy piece of shit? I'll tell you. Richie told me instead of Julius you wanted to use some other computer expert, somebody with 'em bullshit credentials, 'cause that jerk-off at the lawyer license thing scared the shit outa you at that prehearing thing when he says to you and Richie that what Julius knows ain't legit 'cause he ain't got some friggin' piece of paper that's supposed to prove somethin'."

I say, "Well, it was important to establish to the satisfaction of the Disciplinary Committee that there is such a device capable of taking information from my computer and to use what was extracted from my computer to create a clone of it."

"You know, you idiot, here in Brooklyn smarts's one thing, loyalty's another. Julius's part of our team. Our team sinks or swims together. You ain't could disrespect a member of the team, which you wudda done to Julius, who ain't done shit to deserve bein' disrespected.

"So the fuck what he ain't got parents dumb enough to waste over a hundred grand to send him away for four years or whatever to sleep 'til the afternoon, drink 'til his liver's almost wrecked, and then take his sweet time learnin' what Julius learnt on his own in no time.

"I know Richie told you that I ain't gonna spring to pay for no other computer expert, but money had nuttin' to do with it. And it ain't even 'cause I had it all worked out and we ain't even need no computer expert. The reason was we stand by our team through thick and thin. If we go down, we go down together swingin'. That's life and if you wanna be part of this team, you gotta know and play by the rules that we run by here in Brooklyn. Rule number one is loyalty.

"And to make sure you understand what I'm sayin' to you, even if Julius on his own says it's okay for you to get somebody else who has that nice, fancy paper, the right thing for you to tell Julius wudda been: 'Thanks, but no thanks. I don't give a shit if those law license folks don't think you know what you know. I know you do and there ain't no way I'm gonna let nobody disrespect you.' That's what you wudda, shudda said.

"And if you lose your law license 'cause of this, it ain't no different from drawin' a lousy hand in cards. Life goes on and you keep playin', hopin' and prayin' that one day you finally draw a card that gives you a winnin' hand. When you lose, you ain't the only one who hadda deal with hard knocks. You just gotta pick your ass up and keep fightin'. Just like poor or sick folks do, and just like lots of blacks in this country gotta do every single day of their lives; like all 'em migrants do, runnin' away from the shit that's goin' on in their countries lookin' for a better place and life for their families. Your white skin ain't mean you ain't gonna suffer in this life. In fact, sufferin' does us all some good; helps us understand what lots of other folks gotta deal with and teaches us somethin' about the true meanin' of this life."

Wow!

◆

THERESA RETURNS HOME a short time after this mess is finally resolved and all the stolen money is back where each penny belongs.

Peace reigns between me and my clients, my reputation is restored, and Caroline is now happy to come to work, as my practice is just about back to normal.

As it turns out, to my great shock, Theresa knows about every single thing that had occurred while she was away. Unbeknownst to me, Julius had installed the WhatsApp

app on her phone, and this permitted her to chat regularly with Mick, who filled her in with a blow-by-blow account of what had happened with those Charter Bank accounts.

Before she left on her trip, Theresa told me that it was unlikely that there would be any phone connection between Brooklyn and many of the places she planned to visit. We did talk several times when she arrived in Japan for the first leg of her trip, but once this thing with my Charter Bank accounts happened, I stopped hearing from her. I assumed this was due to weak phone signal connections.

As it turns out, Mick instructed her not to call me and not to answer her phone if I called her. They both knew that if she and I talked during this fiasco, it would have compounded the tremendous pressure I was under dealing with this mysterious mess. Mick kept her in the loop and assured her every step of the way not to worry that he would make sure everything worked out in the end.

She told me, "I just trusted that it would get fixed, because Mick said it would. My being here or on top of this from afar would not have helped in any way. So, I stayed away until Mick said it was the right time for me to return. In particular, I knew you would never let Mary and Roger down. Mick, I knew, never would permit that either.

"Anyway, it is nice to finally be back home with my sweetie."

I assure her that the feeling is mutual.

Acknowledgements

WRITING A BOOK is said to be a solitary venture. This is certainly true, but only to a certain extent. At just about every step of the way, a writer needs the assistance of others.

So, first, I must thankfully recognize and acknowledge those—too numerous to mention—whose encouragement assisted me to get to the finish line with *Where's ... Eli?*

Then, I must acknowledge Thomas Hinchen, Neil McGuffin, Lisa Talma and Sue Wilson, my beta readers, who agreed to read, and provide feedback about, *Where's ... Eli?*'s initial manuscript. I must single out Tom Hinchen, my brother-in-law who recently retired from teaching grammar school English for over 40 years, who provided me with pages of typos and grammatical errors. Tom also corrected my Spanish words and got me to include the missing tildes and accent marks.

This time around, rather than rely solely on my sister, Sr. Antonina Avitabile, M.S.C., for the correct spellings of the Neapolitan words and expressions sprinkled throughout *Where's ... Eli?*, I took advantage of her trip to Ischia (Italy) to visit our cousin, Raffaele Delfranco, and Raffaele thankfully corrected the previous (mostly incorrect) spellings of those words and expressions. This is why the same words are spelled differently in *Where's ... Eli?* from *Occupational Hazard*. Given the ease of global electronic communication these days, one may wonder—just as I did in retrospect—why I didn't tap Raffaele the first time around. The answer to that is: the ramifications of the world being as small as it now is still hasn't fully sunk in. That's true at least as far as I am concerned.

Once again, I am immensely grateful to my editor Linda Hetzer for her detailed and meticulous editing of *Where's … Eli?* There is more about Linda in my website; be sure to check it out.

While he did not have a hand in assisting me to write my books, this person certainly has rendered meaningful (and greatly appreciated) assistance in spreading the word about both of them. I refer to my Web Master, Jerome McLain of Maxmedia Studios, who created and manages my books' website (http://AlandMickForte.com or https://AlandMickForte.net). For information about Jerome and his firm, go to: https://gov.maxmediastudios.com/about-us/

I must once again acknowledge the great assistance provided me by 1106 Design, LLC (https://www.1106design.com/) in my self-publishing of *Where's … Eli?* Just like the first time around with *Occupational Hazard,* the folks there—Brooklynite Michele DeFilippo and Ronda Rollins—have been instrumental in getting this book ready to roll in no time. 1106 Design handled everything from cover design, final proof reading, interior design, preparing the book's files for print on demand (POD) and eBook, and dealing with Amazon and IngramSpark. 1106 Design's services were invaluable and made the process smooth and easy for me.

And, finally, a shout out to my photographers Ron Jordan Natoli and Steve Warham of Ron Jordan Natoli Studio, located in the heart of Carroll Gardens, Brooklyn. I never knew it was possible for me to look so good. Ron and Steve are creative geniuses.

About the Author

ALEX S. AVITABILE wrote the
Brooklyn tales of his Al and
Mick Forte crime fiction series
after retiring from practicing
law for some 34 years, where
much of his work was for clients
involved in the development of
affordable housing, in New York
City and across the U.S.

Alex grew up and lived most
of his life in what used to be
referred to as South Brooklyn, in
the sections thereof now known as Carroll Gardens and Boerum
Hill. For more information about Alex, go to his website:
http://AlandMickForte.com or https://AlandMickForte.net

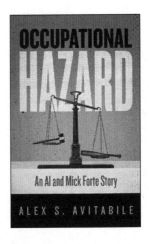

I hope you enjoyed this book.
Would you do me a favor?

Like all authors, I rely on online reviews to encourage future sales. Your opinion is invaluable. Would you take a few moments now to share your assessment of this book—as well as my other book, *OCCUPATIONAL HAZARD*, if (or once) you have read it—on Amazon or any other book review website you prefer? Your opinion will help the book marketplace become more transparent and useful to all.

Thank you very much!

Alex S. Avitabile

Made in the USA
Lexington, KY
09 November 2019